"Load your gun, Troy," Butler said.

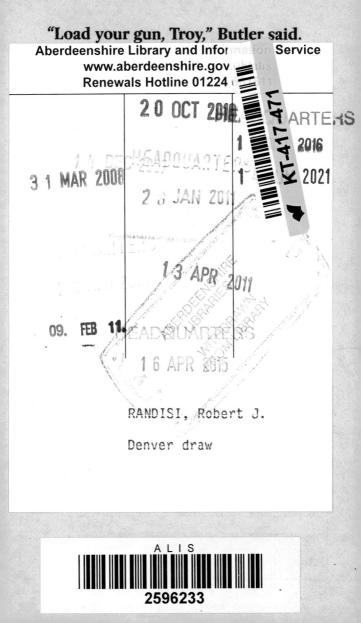

By Robert J. Randisi

THE GAMBLERS

Denver Draw
Butler's Wager

THE SONS OF DANIEL SHAYE

Pearl River Junction
Vengeance Creek
Leaving Epitaph

ROBERT J. RANDISI

THE GAMBLERS
DENVER DRAW

HARPER

An Imprint of HarperCollinsPublishers

This is a wo_____ s are
products of _____ d are
not to be co_____ cales,
organization_____

HARPER

An Imprint of HarperCollins*Publishers*
10 East 53rd Street
New York, New York 10022-5299

Copyright © 2007 by Robert J. Randisi
ISBN: 978-0-06-089020-9
ISBN-10: 0-06-089020-7

First Harper paperback printing: October 2007

THE GAMBLERS
DENVER DRAW

CHAPTER 1

———◆———

Leadville, CO

"Tyrone Butler?" Frank Rode asked.

"That's right."

"Say, weren't you involved in that whole Dodge City mess a while back?" he asked.

"What mess?" Billy Brookens asked.

"You know, that shootout in the plaza thing," Chase said. "It was in the newspapers."

"I remember that," Pete Brand said.

Ty Butler looked at the other four players at the table. None of the four were particularly good poker players and this was a good reason why. None of them were paying attention to the hand.

"Comin' out," Butler, the dealer, said. He ignored their questions and their conversation.

"Jack, no help . . . three, too bad . . . pair of kings on the table . . . a queen for the dealer."

Brookens bet his kings, tossing ten dollars into the pot.

Rode called.

Butler called.

Brand frowned at the three on the table with his eight and ten, all unsuited, but he called. He always called, no matter what he had. It worked in his favor once in a while, but mostly he just tossed good money after bad.

Leadville had been easy pickings for Butler, who was planning to leave the next morning. He'd built up a nice poke, plus he'd rested up enough after the whole Dodge City fiasco that the others were talking about. Standing side-by-side in the streets of Dodge with Bat and Jim Masterson, not to mention Neal Brown, had been invigorating, but everything leading up to it had been tiring. Yet he now felt renewed and ready to travel again. Leadville had been a good place to recuperate, both mentally and physically.

"That dust-up in Dodge was nothin' compared to what happened in Tombstone right after that," Rode said.

"I heard Masterson ran out on the Earps and left them and Doc Holliday to do the dirty work," Brand said.

"I heard a lot of things about Bat Masterson," Brookens said, "but never that he was a coward."

"First time for everything," Rode said.

Butler held his tongue and dealt out the fifth and final card. A queen joined his other queen on the table. He had one in the hole. He felt he had the winning hand, but that was nothing new. Brookens had kings on the table, but Butler had a read on the man. That was all he had. It was more likely that Brand had lucked into three threes by staying in. It was going to cost him money. Rode was out of it, and demonstrated so by folding.

Brookens bet his kings, Butler raised, and Brand foolishly reraised. With two raisers Brookens knew his kings were no food and went out.

"I raise again," Butler said.

The kid had three threes. He could see it on his face. Nine times out of ten that was a winning hand. This was ten but the kid wouldn't consider that.

"I'm puttin' the rest of my money in against you, Mr. Butler," he said, pushing his cash into the center of the table.

It wasn't much because he had been losing all night, but it was all he had. Butler covered the bet.

"I got three treys, Mr. Butler," Brand said. "Can you beat that?"

Butler turned over his third queen.

"What's wrong with you, boy?" Rode, the oldest player at the table, asked. "Ain't you been watchin' this man play all night?"

Pete Brand looked as if he was going to cry. Finally, he just pushed his chair back, got up, and went to the bar.

Butler collected his chips.

Rode gathered the cards to deal.

"The kid was probably wrong about Bat Masterson bein' a coward, too," Brookens said.

"He was," Butler said.

Brookens and Rode looked at him.

"Bat left Tombstone to go to Dodge to keep his brothers alive," Butler said. "That's why he wasn't at the O.K. Corral. And any man who says different is going to have to deal with me."

Rode shuffled the cards and kept quiet. Brookens opened his mouth to speak, then thought better of it.

"Way I heard it," a voice from the bar called out, "Masterson didn't even go to Dodge. He just plumb lit out from Tombstone and kept goin' until he reached Trinidad, and he's a-hidin' out there."

Butler didn't know the voice. He turned to see who the speaker was. The man was in his early thirties, was holding a mug of beer and smirking for the benefit of his friends standing at the bar with him, of which there were three.

"That's Troy Smithson, Butler," Frank Rode said to him. "Don't let him goad you into a gunfight. He's fast."

"I know about Smithson, Frank," Butler said. "I've been here long enough for that."

"Then you know to ignore him," Billy Brookens said. "Come on, gentlemen. Let's play cards."

But Troy Smithson was not easily ignored. During the time Butler had been in Leadville—close to a month—Smithson had goaded or called out three men and killed them all in a "fair" fight. The town laws—such as it was—turned its head because Smithson worked for one of the largest mine owners in Colorado. He wasn't a miner, he was more of a bodyguard, or enforcer.

Apparently, now that he had heard Butler's word about Bat Masterson, he'd decided that Ty Butler would be his next victim.

CHAPTER 2

Smithson kept talking about Bat Masterson, questioning not only his courage but his manhood as well.

Butler lost the next hand because he couldn't concentrate. If he didn't shut this idiot up, he'd have to stop playing.

"Deal me out this hand," Butler said.

"Just this hand?" Rode asked.

"One hand." Butler nodded.

He stood up, turned, and walked to the bar, where Smithson was holding court with his friends. The man had a decided height and weight advantage on Butler, but the gambler did not intend to fight with him.

"Can I help you?" Smithson asked.

"I can only assume that you're trying to annoy me with all this talk about Bat Masterson."

"He a friend of yours?"

"More of an acquaintance," Butler said. "I'm actually friends with Jim Masterson."

"Jim?" Smithson laughed. "He got run out of Dodge, didn't he? With his tail between his legs?"

"Well," Butler said, "whatever you think of the Mastersons, that's not why I'm here."

"Why are you here," Smithson asked, "in my face, where you don't belong?"

"I'm playing in a poker game over there," Butler said, "and you're interfering with my concentration."

"That penny ante game?"

The stakes were higher than that, but that wasn't the point.

"Yes, that game," Butler said. "I'll give you two bits to go away." Butler took the twenty-five cents out of his pocket.

"Two bits?" one of Smithson's friends asked, laughing.

"That all yer worth, Troy?" another one asked.

"I'm only offering two bits," Butler said, clarifying the point, "because I don't have a plugged nickel on me."

The room took notice of what was going on at the bar and suddenly it got very quiet.

"Jesus, Troy," Friend #1 said, "he's sayin' you ain't even worth a plugged nickel."

"That ain't what he's sayin', ya idjit," Friend #2 said. "He's sayin' Troy *is* worth a plugged nickel."

Both men started to laugh.

"Shut up!" Smithson snapped.

Both men did.

"That what you're sayin', friend?" Smithson demanded. "I'm worth a plugged nickel?"

"Did I say a plugged nickel?" Butler asked. "Maybe just a regular nickel, but whichever it is I'm offering you a whole quarter."

There was some laughter from the room, but when Smithson looked around it stopped.

"Mister, are you tryin' ta make a fool outta me?" he demanded pugnaciously.

"You don't need my help for that, friend."

Smithson frowned, still not sure what was going on.

"I tell you what," Butler said. "How about I buy you and your friends beer and you just shut your mouth?"

"Hey, that sounds good to me, Troy," Friend #1 said.

"Shut up, Pete," Smithson said, and then turned his attention back to Butler. "Mister, you know who I am?"

"I've got a pretty good idea what you are," Butler said. "Who you are doesn't really matter to me."

Smithson puffed out his chest and said, "It better matter to you, if you know what's good fer ya."

"Troy," Friend #2 said, "maybe we oughtta—"

"Maybe you oughtta just shut the hell up, Dusty," Smithson suggested forcefully.

His friend, Pete Brand, and Dusty Rich, knew when Troy Smithson was on the edge, so they decided to take his advice and shut up. They didn't want to become the targets for his anger. They'd leave that to the gambler, who obviously did not know who he was dealing with.

"What do you say, fella?" Ty Butler asked. "You want to take that free beer?"

"I don't want no beer from you, friend," Smithson said. "I want you out in the street."

"Now?"

"Right now."

"Getting dark out there," Butler said, looking out the front window. "You sure?"

"It's light enough for me ta kill you."

"Okay, then," Butler said. "You go ahead, I'll be right out soon as I make sure my money is safe."

Smithson looked at the other two.

"You guys stay here," he said. "This won't take long."

With that Troy Smithson stormed outside into the street to await Butler's arrival. Everyone in the room expected Butler to collect his money and follow the man out. Instead, all Butler did was turn around, return to his table, and reclaim his seat.

"I thought he'd never leave," he said. "Deal me in, boys."

CHAPTER 3

It took Smithson's friends a few minutes before they realized Butler was not going to go outside. They exchanged a glance and then walked over to the table.

"Uh, Mister?" Dusty asked.

"Yes?" Butler replied.

"You do know that Troy is waitin' for ya outside, right?"

"I know that."

"Uh . . . ain't you gonna go out?"

"Not if I can help it."

"B-but," Pete Brand said, "he called you out."

Butler looked up at both of them.

"And you think that means I have to go out?"

"Well . . . yeah," Brand said.

"Forget it," Butler said. "I've got a hot hand going here, boys. I ain't about to walk away from this game."

"B-but . . . Troy's gonna be mad," Dusty said.

"Let him get mad. What do I care?"

"Mister . . . he'll kill ya," Brand said.

"He's right, Butler," one of the other poker players said. "Smithson's mean and you're just makin' him meaner by leavin' him standin' out there."

"He'll come in here and shoot up the place," another card player added.

"Where's the sheriff when you need him?" Butler asked.

"You been in Leadville long enough to know Sheriff Galloway ain't worth shit, Butler," the first player said. "You got 'im riled up, you're gonna have to deal with him."

Butler looked around the table. All of the players were staring at him and nodding, as well as some of the on-lookers.

"You fellas don't care one way or the other who gets killed, do you?" he asked. "Just so long as he doesn't come in here shooting and interrupt the game."

"I care," one of the players said.

The others looked at him,

"Hey, Butler's got most of my money," he complained. "I want a chance to get it back."

"Can't much blame you for that," Butler said. He looked around at Smithson's two friends. "Go and tell your buddy I'll be out directly."

"He's probably pretty mad as it is," Dusty said.

"He might shoot the first man comes out the door," Brand said.

"Then you better make sure he knows it's you," Butler replied, "hadn't you?"

"Uh, yeah, sure," Brand said, "okay."

The two men went to the batwing doors and then cautiously stepped outside.

"Sounds like you all want me to do this?" Butler said.

The men around the table nodded; onlookers did just that.

Butler sighed.

"You realize this means I'll have to kill him?"

"You could go out the back door," someone said. "Leave town."

Butler sat back. The game had been ruined for him, and he had intended to leave Leadville the next day, anyway. Going out the back door had some merit.

"That'd be the coward's way out," another voice said. "Go on out and kill 'im. He's a tin gun anyway, always lookin' ta hire out and prove himself."

That's when it occurred to Butler that this might be something totally different.

"Ya ain't got a price on yer head, does ya?" somebody asked.

Actually, he did, though not a lawfully placed one. Could Smithson have been trying to goad him into a fight in order to collect?

Suddenly, going out the back door didn't seem like such a good idea.

"I'm cashing out," he announced.

"Ain't comin' back even if you kill him?" a player asked.

"No," Butler said. "I'm done with the game, and done with Leadville. I'll be leaving in the morning."

"If'n you ain't dead tonight," somebody said.

He looked around but could not pick out the man who had spoken.

Outside Troy Smithson said to his two friends, "So, do you think he bought it?"

"He bought it," Dusty said. "He'll be comin' out thinkin' he's only got to face you."

"Good."

"You was real good in there, Troy," Brand said. "I thought you was really losin' your temper."

Smithson glared at Brand and said, "I was. I hate that gambler. Thinks he's so much better'n us."

"Well, he's gonna learn different," Dusty said.

"Yeah, he is," Smithson said. "He sure is. Check your guns, boys. We're about to make us some money."

They fanned out in front of the hotel, checked their loads, holstered their guns, and waited.

In the end, Butler did decide to go out the back door. In spite of the jeers and barbs that were fired at him by the patrons of the saloon, it turned out to be an excellent idea.

CHAPTER 4

Butler moved down alongside the saloon until he reached the street. Sure enough, standing out in front of the saloon were the three friends, fanned out and waiting for him. It had all been an act, designed to lure him outside, convinced that he would only be facing one man, Troy Smithson.

He drew his gun, briefly considered taking two of them right then and there, leaving the third to be questioned. Try as he might, though, he couldn't convince himself to shoot them from hiding. He was not a bushwacker, and holstered his weapon.

He stepped out of the alley, up onto the boardwalk. It was a dark night, with a sliver of a moon and almost no stars. Leadville's streets were not well lit. The three men had been outside long enough for their eyes to adjust, but they were waiting for him to step out of the lighted saloon. If he had done that he probably would not have even noticed there were three men until it was too late. But from the shadows it was he who would be able to see, and they who would be blind.

"You boys put on a good act," he called out.

All three men were startled, began glancing around to see where the voice had come from.

"That you, Butler?" Smithson said. "Come out where I can see you."

"You 'mean come out where you can all gun me down," Butler said. "I don't think so."

"Whataya talkin' about?" Smithson asked. "This is just between you and me."

"That a fact? Then suppose you tell your buddies to drop their guns in the street and walk away? Then I'll come out and face you, just you and me."

Smithson didn't answer right away. The other two looked at him, then at each other.

"They'll walk away," Smithson said. "That oughtta be good enough."

"No," Butler said. "It's not."

Finally, Smithson seemed to locate him, staring into the shadows, so Butler moved a few feet to his left.

"There!" Smithson shouted, pointing with his left hand and drawing his gun with his right. "He's there. Get him!"

All three men drew and began firing where Smithson was pointing. By that time Butler had moved even further to the left and stepped into a doorway, putting him even deeper in shadow. The fact that the three men were firing also freed him to do the same without any guilt about firing from cover.

He drew and shot Dusty through the chest. As the man fell onto his back in the street, the other two men trained their weapons on Butler's muzzle flash, but Butler was moving again . They fired, glass began breaking, and now Butler was in the street with them. He fired a second time, taking Pete Brand in the hip. The impact spun him around and Butler's next shot struck him in the back. Brand fell on his face.

It was quiet. Butler and Smithson were standing in the street, alone. Patrons from the saloon had crowded around the door and windows to watch.

"Holster it," Butler said. "Or we can both start firing."

Smithson stared at him.

"I'm . . . I'm empty."

"That's because you wasted a lot of lead breaking windows."

"You gonna kill me?" Smithson asked.

"That's up to you."

"Whataya mean?"

"Who sent you?"

Smithson looked confused, asked again, "Whataya mean?"

"Load your gun, Troy."

"But I—"

"Go ahead, load it," Butler said. "I'm not about to shoot an unarmed man."

If Smithson had been smart he would have dropped his gun in the street upon hearing Butler's declaration. But he wasn't smart. He ejected the spent shells from his gun, and then slowly began to reload from his gun belt.

"Okay, now holster it."

Smithson stood stock-still, gun in hand, but pointed down toward the street.

"Don't even think about it, Troy," Butler said. "Holster it."

Grudgingly, Smithson did as he was told.

"Now I'm going to ask you again," Butler said. "Who sent you and your partners after me?"

"Nobody sent us," the other man said. "We heard there was paper out on you."

"Are you bounty hunters?"

"No."

"Then why come after me."

"There's a lot of money on your head."

"Put there by who?"

"Hell, I dunno," Smithson said. "How would I know? All I know is what the paper says."

"Where's the paper now?"

"I dunno," he said. "Dusty had it."

"You don't know a hell of a lot, do you, Troy?" Butler asked. "Except that I was worth money to you dead."

Smithson shrugged and said, "Nothing personal, Butler."

"Really? I take somebody trying to kill me very personal," Butler said. He holstered his own gun.

"Now's your chance, Troy."

"Huh?"

"Go ahead," Butler said. "Earn your money."

Smithson continued to look confused.

"Come on, Troy," Butler said. "Make a move, either draw your gun or walk away."

Butler kept a wary eye on Smithson. By now they were both able to see each other equally well. Butler was able to make out the expression on Smithson's face. Even as the man started to turn, as if to walk away, Butler knew he was going to try it.

When Smithson went for his gun, turning back, hoping to catch Butler unaware, he was surprised to find Butler ready for him. The gambler drew and shot him in the chest twice. He figured the man deserved one bullet for his deceit and one for his stupidity.

"Hold it!"

Butler turned and saw Sheriff Galloway walking toward him with his gun out.

"Sheriff, you better holster that or use it."

"What?" Galloway, a tall man in his thirties with a straggly goatee, stopped short. "Are you threatening me?"

"No threat," Butler said. "I've just looked down the barrel of enough guns tonight."

"What went on here?" Reluctantly, the lawman holstered his weapon.

"I think you know. I think you watched and waited for it to be all over."

"I need to know what went on, here," Galloway repeated lamely.

"Ask them," Butler said, pointing to the men in the saloon, still peering out the windows and the door. "They'll tell you. I'm going to bed."

Butler holstered his gun and started to walk away, then turned back.

"Oh, and I'll be gone by morning . . . and not a minute too soon to suit me."

CHAPTER 5

Trinidad, Colorado

Bat Masterson stepped out of his office and looked up and down the street. When he had first come to Trinidad some months ago, he hadn't intended to stay long. He certainly hadn't intended to become town marshal. The incident he privately referred to as "The Debacle in Dodge City," had left him with a bad taste in his mouth. Not to mention the fact that leaving Tombstone to go to Dodge to help his brother Jim meant he hadn't been at the O.K. Corral to help the Earps and Doc Holliday. From what he'd heard, even though that shootout had happened some time ago, Wyatt and Doc were still hunting some of those cowboys down. Apparently, Wyatt was intent on his revenge for the crippling of one of his brothers—Virgil—and the murder of the other, Morgan.

Trinidad was fairly quiet, especially since Bat had taken over as sheriff, and even in a position of authority it seemed to be a place where Bat could relax, lay back, and take stock.

So far, he hadn't decided much, and all that was

ahead of him today was what to have for breakfast, and where.

He stepped down from the boardwalk, crossed the street, and began walking toward a nearby restaurant, exchanging greetings with some of the townspeople, all of whom were very grateful that Bat Masterson was the marshal of Trinidad.

Butler was close enough to Trinidad to have ridden in the night before, but he decided to camp first and then ride in come morning. He wasn't sure how Bat Masterson was going to greet him. Masterson didn't know that it was Butler who had sent him the telegram, telling him that his brother Jim was in danger in Dodge. It was that telegram that drew Bat away from Tombstone before all hell broke loose there. Jim Masterson actually was in danger in Dodge, and Bat's arrival in Dodge did set off the shootout—which Butler was part of—that resulted in all the parties—the surviving parties—leaving town. Bat had not been happy with what had happened, and Butler decided never to tell him that he'd sent the telegram. But even not knowing that, Bat might not be glad to see him in Trinidad.

Still, he intended to ride in and test the waters. He'd been out of Leadville for a few days now, and was looking for a place to stop for a while, maybe just a few days, before continuing west. He'd been on his way to California when he heard about Leadville, and his detour there had been profitable, but he was now ready to head west again. All he had to do was outfit himself in Trinidad and he'd be on his way.

He woke that morning and decided to have breakfast in town, so he broke camp without so much as a pot of coffee, mounted up, and headed for town. He had his fingers crossed that Bat Masterson would not run him out of town as soon as he saw him.

•

Masterson had decided on a place for breakfast, a restaurant a couple of blocks from his office. He was about to go inside when he heard a horse coming down the street. It wasn't an unusual sound, but for some reason this morning he stopped to have a look.

The rider looked familiar from a distance. He was clad in a black gambler's suit, white shirt, and black flat-brimmed hat. Bat waited until he got closer, then stepped down into the street to intercept him.

"Never thought I'd see you again so soon," he said to Tyrone Butler.

"I was in Leadville," Butler said. "I just need a couple of days to rest up and then I'm on my way to California."

"What's there?"

"Poker, I hope."

"We got poker here."

"I heard."

"Step down, Butler," Bat said. "I was about to have breakfast inside here." He indicated the restaurant they were in front of.

"Any good?"

"Long as you don't want nothin' fancy."

"Just a hot breakfast's all I want."

"Dismount, then," Bat said. "We never did get to know each other in Dodge."

Butler, surprised by Masterson's reaction, said, "Much obliged, Bat," and did as he was invited to do.

CHAPTER 6

———◦◉◦———

Inside the restaurant Bat sat with his back to the wall, leaving Butler to sit uncomfortably across from him.

"Don't worry," Bat said. "I'll watch your back. Least I can do after what you did for my brother."

"I didn't do much."

"Jim and I talked after the Dodge City thing was over," Bat said. "You and me, we didn't get a chance to talk. He told me you saved his life."

"Well . . ."

A middle-aged woman came to the table then and said, "'mornin', Marshal. What'll ya have?"

"Steak and eggs, Maggie, what else? Butler?"

"The same."

"Coffee?" Maggie asked.

Butler looked at Bat.

"The sheriff always has coffee," she said.

"Then I'll have some, too."

"Thanks, Maggie."

Butler looked around.

"I know," Bat said. "It's empty. Word gets around where I'm havin' breakfast and the place stays empty till I'm done."

"That the way you want it?"

"Naw," Bat said, "but that's the way it is. When you got a rep with a gun, folks don't want to be around you much. And if you're wearin' a badge, that goes double."

"Folks like Maggie don't mind?"

"Nobody minds. They like havin' me here as sheriff. Eatin' breakfast somewhere else is a small price to pay."

"What made you come here after Dodge?"

"Didn't come straight here, but ended up here," Bat said. "They needed a marshal, I needed a place to stay for a while. Also got a faro layout in one of the saloons, so I'm doin' pretty well. Where'd you go after Dodge?"

"Here and there. Ended up in Leadville for a little while."

"I heard a gambler killed three men in Leadville some time ago," Bat said. "That you?"

"That was me."

"Three on one?"

"I had an advantage."

"What was that?"

"They were all stupid."

"Guess you and me'd have that advantage over most folks I've met," Bat said.

Maggie came over with the coffee and promised the plates soon.

"She'll get 'em out here quick so I'll eat and skedaddle," Bat said.

"I'll eat quick," Butler offered. "I've got to get my horse seen to and get myself a room."

"I got some rooms over in my saloon," Bat said. "You can have one if you want."

"On what condition?" Butler asked, wondering if Bat had a table or actually owned a piece of the place.

Bat smiled.

"Hey, you are smart. I need a relief dealer. You do that for me and you can have the room free."

"Can't make myself much money if I'm dealing for the house."

"I'll pay ya."

"I can make more playing poker for myself."

"So play poker for yourself," Bat said. "Don't play nowhere else in town and you can still have the room. But you can also relieve me when I need it. You can deal faro, can't you?"

"Sure, but let me get this straight. You want me to play exclusively in your place? And relieve you once in a while at your faro table, Butler asked. "That's all you want?"

"That's it. Sounds cushy to me. We got a deal?"

"For how long?" Butler asked.

"Long as you want," Bat said. "I get the feeling you and me ain't long for this town, anyway."

Bat stuck his hand out and Butler shook it.

"You got a deal."

"And we got breakfast," Bat said, sitting back as Maggie laid down the large plates of steaming food. "Eat up."

They caught up a bit more during breakfast, but in the back of his head Butler was wondering why Bat was being so friendly to him? True, he had saved Jim Masterson's life, and he stood beside both Masterson brothers in a firefight, but he and Bat didn't exchange two words afterward, and then everybody—Bat, Jim, Neal Brown, and Butler—got into the wind and were gone.

But Bat's offer was too good to pass up.

And he was right about the breakfast. It had been real

good. Both men finished about the same time and left the restaurant.

"There's a livery right down the street," Bat said. "After you get your horse taken care of, come back out to the main street and make a left. My place is two blocks down on the right."

"What's it called?"

"The Bonanza," Bat said.

"You going to be there when I get there?" Butler asked.

"I've got to make some rounds, but I'll end up there. Don't worry, you'll have a room waitin'. Got some pretty gals workin' there, too. You can have your pick."

"That come with the job?"

Bat laughed and said, "That's gonna be up to them."

CHAPTER 7

The Bonanza was impressive. It looked to be fashioned after saloons Butler had seen in places like Wichita, Ellsworth, and Dodge City. He stepped through the batwing doors, carrying his saddlebags and rifle, and stopped just inside. It was all glass and wood paneling, the bar—if not the longest in the west, very close—looked like cherrywood. The paintings on the wall were all of voluptuous women in the nude. Butler recognized the artist as Peter Paul Rubens and wondered if any of them were originals.

It was early and the place was empty, obviously not yet open for business. There were two bartenders preparing the bar for when they did open. All of the gaming tables were covered.

Standing at the bar was Bat Masterson, drinking a cup of coffee.

"Come on in, Butler," Bat called. "Whataya think of the place?"

"It's amazing," Butler said, joining Bat at the bar.

"Drink? Coffee?"

"Coffee'd be good." It was a drink Butler could never have enough of.

Bat waved at one of the bartenders who gave him a refill and Butler a fresh cup.

"This is Roscoe, our head bartender," Bat said. "That's Willy."

Roscoe, a ruddy-faced man in his thirties, nodded. Willy, ten years younger and fresh-faced, waved.

"Willy's in training," Bat added.

"Where's your table?" Butler asked.

"In the corner, back there." Bat used his chin to point.

"When do you take the cover off."

"I've got one deputy," Bat said. "When he comes on duty I open the table up. With you here, though, I can open earlier and stay open later."

"I've got to admit, it's been a while since I dealt faro," Butler said.

"You never forget," Bat said, nodding. "The one thing Neal Brown told me about you in Dodge was that you were a good card player."

"Poker player."

Bat waved.

"Cards are cards," Bat said. "I'm not worried. Nobody in this town plays that well."

"Still . . ."

"You want me to brief you on the layout?"

"It couldn't hurt."

"Why don't you put your gear in your room," Bat said. "Up the stairs, second door. I'll meet you at the table."

Butler went up. There were only rooms on one side, with a railing overlooking the saloon on the other. On a busy night, if he was in his room trying to sleep, he was sure he'd be able to hear the racket. That wouldn't keep him awake, though. On the contrary, the murmur of voices—or even shouts—and the clatter of chips would lull him to sleep.

The room was fine. Simple, clean, better than some, worse than others. He dropped his saddlebags on the bed, set his rifle down in a corner, and went back downstairs.

Bat had the cover off his faro table. The green felt had faded some, but the symbols were sharp. Bat only needed ten minutes to bring Butler up to date before covering the table again.

"You'll be fine," he said to Butler.

"Bat, how long have you been the law here?"

"About four months."

"And how much longer do you see yourself wearing that badge?"

"As long as my luck holds out on this table," he said. "When the cards start to run bad, that's when I'll put out. Or whenever I get antsy."

Butler understood that. He'd experienced that feeling himself many times.

They went back to the bar and got their coffees freshened, this time by Willy.

"Say," Bat said then, "you wouldn't be interested in wearin' a badge, would you? I could always use another deputy."

"I don't think so."

"You can obviously handle a gun. From what I heard happened in Leadville, and what I saw in Dodge, you're better than most."

"Not in your league."

"Hell, as long as you can hit what you aim at—"

"I don't think I'd be interested in being a faro dealer and a deputy, Bat. Too time-consuming. I'd never have time for poker."

"Yeah, I can see that," Bat said. "And I need you more as a dealer than a deputy."

Butler was relieved. He didn't want to insult Bat in any way. He still didn't know the man very well, and wasn't sure what kind of temper he had. He'd heard some stories, didn't know if they were true, and didn't want to test them out.

"We're good, then," he said.

"If you want to play poker tonight until about ten and then relieve me, that's fine," Bat said. "I make late rounds about then."

"Ten it will be, then."

Bat put his cup down.

"I'll see you then." He waved at both the bartenders and left. When he was gone Willy came over, cleaning a glass.

"You friends with Mr. Masterson?"

"More like acquaintances."

"He don't usually let nobody touch his layout," the young bartender said. "He must think you're friends."

"Maybe so," Butler said. "I'd be honored if he did."

Willy was about to say more when Roscoe shouted for him.

"Gotta go," he said.

Butler didn't think of himself and Bat as friends—not yet, anyway—but what had happened in Dodge had apparently given him some respect in the eyes of Bat Masterson, and that pleased him.

CHAPTER 8

About a week's ride out of Trinidad three riders were camped. Sharing coffee around the fire. They were on their way into town, but in no particular hurry.

"Feels odd," Virgil said.

"What does?" Wyatt asked.

"The feeling that we're not . . . huntin' anybody."

"Or bein' hunted," Doc said.

"That's your thing, Doc," Virgil said. "We never been hunted."

"Sure you have," Doc said. "Maybe you just didn't notice it."

Despite the fact that Doc Holliday had stood with the Earps against the Clantons and cowboys, Virgil still didn't trust him, or even like him much. Doc was Wyatt's friend. There was never any pretense about that. Doc had stood with Wyatt, not with the law, and not with the Earps.

"Morgan was sure bein' hunted that night," Doc added.

He was talking about the night in Tombstone that Morgan Earp had been shot and killed.

"Don't talk about Morg, Doc," Virgil warned the tubercular killer.

"Why not?" Doc asked, narrowing his eyes. "Are you warnin' me off, Virgil?"

"Cut it out, the two of you," Wyatt said. "You're stir crazy and you're drivin' me crazy. We best get into Trinidad where we can be around other people, maybe get away from each other for a little while."

"Suits me," Virgil said, glaring at Doc.

"You sayin' you wanna get away from me?" Doc demanded. "'cause that can be arranged."

Wyatt gave up.

"I'm gonna saddle up my horse," he said. "You two can fight over who breaks camp."

He walked away from them and started to saddle his horse. They were the closest people to him in the world, but the two men were driving him crazy. They'd been riding together so long, just the three of them, that he really needed this stop off in Trinidad—if for no other reason than to see Bat Masterson. He had not seen his friend since he'd left Tombstone to go to Dodge City in response to an anonymous telegram. As it turned out Bat had actually arrived in time to back his brother Jim up in a fight. After that things had exploded in Tombstone, and Wyatt had been too busy to correspond with Bat. So this visit was overdue.

And, of course, there was the fact that there were some warrants out for the Earps and Doc, and maybe Bat—seeing as he was wearing a star—might be able to help.

Virgil and Doc watched Wyatt walk over to where they had picketed the horses.

"He needs some rest," Virgil said.

"I know."

"And we're drivin' him crazy."

Virgil looked at Doc.

"Yeah, I know," he said, "and each other."

"We need to be around some other people, I guess," Doc said. "People who aren't tryin' to kill us."

"Right."

"I'll get the fire," Doc said.

"I'll saddle your horse and mine," Virgil said.

"Thanks."

"Sure."

Virgil walked over to where Wyatt was saddling his own horse.

Doc poured the remnants of the coffeepot onto the fire and then stamped it out. He felt a cough coming on, but was able to quell it for the moment. He was running out of kerchiefs that didn't have blood on them.

He looked over at the Earp brothers. He knew the two of them were hurtin' over the death of their brother, Morgan, and Virgil had one arm that wasn't much good to him. He wondered what the brothers were going to decide to do after Trinidad. They hadn't talked about the future much. They'd managed to track down as many of the cowboys as they could and had left them for dead. He didn't know what else was on the Earp agenda, but he had a life of his own to lead.

What was left of it.

"Hey, Wyatt," Virgil said. "Doc and I are sorry."

"Yeah," Wyatt said, leaning on his horse, "I'm sorry, too. I guess we're all just tired."

"Tired of each other."

"Yeah."

They both turned and looked at Doc.

"I'm kinda worried about Doc, though," Wyatt said.

"I know," Virgil said, "that cough of his is gettin' worse. I seen him spittin' up blood a couple of times."

Wyatt said, "Not only that. The warrants against us won't stand up. We were wearin' badges. But if they get Doc back into Arizona and make the charges stick, they might hang 'im."

"Well then," Virgil said, "we better make sure he don't ever go back to Arizona."

"Bat might be able to help," Wyatt said. "He's the marshal in Trinidad. He's gotta have some connections."

Bat Masterson was someone else who was Wyatt's friend, not Virgil's. In fact, Virgil didn't have many friends other than his brothers, Wyatt and Morgan—and now there was only Wyatt.

"Bat and Doc don't get along," Virgil pointed out.

"I don't know too many people who get along with Doc," Wyatt said. "But Bat will help. He won't see Doc railroaded, no matter how he feels about him. I know him that well."

"I hope you're right," Virgil said, "for your sake—"

"You got them horses saddled yet?" Doc called out. "I swear, Virg, you're slowin' down in your old age."

"—And Doc's," Virgil said to Wyatt.

"I'll get your horse," Wyatt said, "you get Doc's."

They walked the horses over to where Doc was waiting and Virgil handed the gunman the reins.

"Thanks. Think your buddy Masterson is gonna be glad to see us?" Doc asked.

"I don't know," Wyatt said. "I guess we better just ride on in and find out, huh?"

CHAPTER 9

———◆◆◆———

Butler played some poker that evening, won a little bit of money while he was trying to gauge the caliber of the other players. He also paid some attention to Bat Masterson's table. Bat did a good business, and from what Butler could tell, took money from all comers.

Earlier in the day Butler had met Bat's deputy, a young man named Dean Collier. He was in his mid-twenties, and seemed to be in total awe of his boss. While Bat was manning his faro table Deputy Collier would come in and out, apparently with questions for his boss. At times Bat would roll his eyes, answer the young man, and send him on his way.

It was almost time for Butler to relieve Bat at his table when Collier came in again. He walked to Bat's table, whispered something that caused Bat to wave his hands and abruptly close his table. He and Collier started for the door, then stopped short. Bat said something to his deputy, then turned and walked to the poker table where Butler was sitting.

"Want me to take your table?" Butler asked, looking up at him.

"How are you doin'?" Bat asked.

"I'm making money but I can get away."

"I don't need you to stand at my table, but I might have need of your gun, if you're a mind to give it."

"Got something you and your deputy can't handle?"

"I might."

Butler didn't need to hear any more. He cashed out of the game and followed Bat to the door.

"Why do we need him?" Collier asked as they stepped outside.

"How many men have you shot at, Dean?"

"Well . . . none."

"Then shut up."

As they started down the street Bat explained to Butler, "We got a saloon at the far end of town—if we were in Dodge it would be in the red-light district. The bartender there sent a runner over to the office to say there was trouble brewin'. At that end of town that usually means shootin'. In the past I've been able to talk these fellas down, but the last time it almost came to gunplay. This time . . ."

"How many men we talkin' about?"

"Probably half a dozen," Bat said. "They're young, and don't think the law applies to them."

"They're not impressed with you?"

Bat gave him a look.

"Not everybody is impressed with me, Butler," he said. "But even if they are, they been buildin' up to tryin' me on for size. I'm guessin' tonight might be the night."

This wasn't what Butler had signed on for, but when Bat Masterson asks you for help you don't refuse.

In the Bucket of Blood saloon, at the far western end of town, six men in their mid twenties, guns in their hands, were holding the entire place hostage.

"Come on, boys," Tom Reed, the owner said. "This has gone far enough, hasn't it?"

"Naw, I don't think it has," Fred Vance said. He was the leader of the other five. They worked only when they had to, took what they wanted when they were drunk enough. Not full-fledged outlaws, but certainly in training. Holding a saloon full of men under their guns seemed to excite all of them.

Reed tried one of the other men.

"Hastings, you got some sense. Talk to Fred—"

Before he could finish Vance stepped forward and backhanded him across the face. Reed, an older man in his late fifties, staggered and almost fell. He wiped his mouth with the back of his own hand and came away with blood.

"You're goin' too far, Reed," he said.

"Ya think so?" Reed asked. "Then go for that gun I know ya got under yer arm, Tom. Go ahead, I dare ya."

"You goddamned young pup," Reed said. "If you didn't have five guns backin' you up—"

"I'll tell them to holster their guns, Tom. That make you any braver?"

Before Reed could answer, Toby Allen called from the door, "Law comin'."

"Masterson?" Reed asked.

Toby nodded. "He's got somebody with him."

"One's his deputy, Collier," Vance said. "He won't be much trouble."

"You'll get all the trouble you want from Bat Masterson, Vance," Reed said.

"You think so?" Vance asked. "There's six of us, Tom."

"That don't matter," Reed said. "Bat's faced better than you, more than you, many times before."

"Yeah, well," Vance said, "maybe this time he's gonna bite off more than he can handle." He turned his attention to the room in general. The tables were full of men who were drinking and playing cards, tables full of men who had no desire to go for their guns. "The first man who touches his gun is dead. Understand?"

"They understand, Vance," Reed said. "We all understand. This is gonna be between you and Bat. That's what you want, ain't it? To prove what a big man you are?"

"You wait and see, Tom," Vance said. "You just wait and see how big a man I am."

"Your father's turnin' over in his grave, Fred."

"My father was yeller to the bone, Tom!" Vance shouted, "That ain't me. That ain't never gonna be me. I ain't gonna grow to a ripe old age with a yeller streak down my back."

"Son," Tom Reed said, wiping blood from his mouth again, "I don't think you're gonna grow to a ripe old age, period.

CHAPTER 10

———◆———

Bat put his hand out to stop their progress.

"What's the matter?" Collier asked.

"Listen."

All three men strained and listened to the night.

"I don't hear nothin'," Collier said.

"That's the point," Butler said. "How many saloons have you been in that are that quiet?"

"Somethin's wrong?" Bat asked. "Dean, I want you to go around back. Try the back door, see if you can get in, and then wait for us to move."

"What do I do when you move, Bat?"

"Just follow my lead, kid," Bat said. "Don't fire your gun unless I do. Got it?"

"I got it, Bat."

"We're gonna give you five minutes to get back there."

Collier nodded and took off on the run.

"You trying to keep him out of harm's way?" Butler asked.

"Let's just say he'll get into less trouble back there." Bat looked at him. "You don't mind, do you?"

"I might, if I knew how many guns we were walking into."

"Yeah, you're right," Bat said. "We shoulda stopped by the office for a couple of shotguns."

"Probably one behind the bar."

"Fat lot of good it does us there."

"You never know."

Bat looked at his watch.

"Two minutes, and then we're goin' in."

Butler nodded, and checked his gun.

"What are they doin', Toby?" Vance asked.

"Just standin' there, Fred."

Vance looked around the room, his gun in his hand.

"Remember what I said," he announced to the room at large. "I can get my gun out faster than any of you."

"Don't worry, Fred," Reed said. "We're all gonna watch."

"Good."

He holstered his gun, and his men gaped at him.

"Come on, put them up," he said. "We don't want Masterson to come in shootin'."

Toby and the other men stared at him, and then one by one they holstered their weapons.

"Now spread out," Vance said. "Masterson won't be able to tell you from the others in here. And nobody move until I do."

His men nodded and began to move about the room, picking their spots and standing ready.

"Time," Bat said.

"How do you want to play this?"

Bat shrugged. "You got somethin' in mind?"

"I'm not wearing a badge," Butler said. "I could go in first."

"If anybody's watchin' they've seen us together by now," Bat said. "Might not make a difference."

"You never know."

Bat thought a moment, then said, "Okay, then, go ahead. Be ready to use that gun, though. These are a bunch of young pups who are on the verge of becomin' wild dogs. Don't let the look of them fool you. None of them looks like they shave yet."

"I'll keep that in mind."

"And whatever happened in there, don't give up your gun."

"I won't," Butler said. "Just give me a couple of minutes and then come ahead."

"I appreciate the backup, Butler."

"Thank me when it's over."

He headed for the saloon.

CHAPTER 11

Butler mounted the boardwalk in front of the Bucket of Blood—how many saloons had he seen with that name in his travels—and entered through the batwing doors. As soon as he entered he felt the tension, realized he was the center of attention.

"What's wrong with that marshal?" Butler asked.

No answer.

"Likes to give people a hard time for no reason?"

"You a stranger in town?" someone asked. He saw that it was a man standing at the bar. He was tall, wore a gun like he knew how to use it—or like someone taught him to wear it. He was in his twenties. Behind him a portly man in his fifties dabbed at a bleeding mouth.

"That's right."

"Marshal's name is Bat Masterson," the man said. "That mean anything to you?"

"I heard of him," Butler said. "Can't say it means anything to me, though. Can I move away from the door now? I'd like to get a beer."

"Get your beer," the man said, "and stay out of trouble."

"Much obliged."

Butler walked to the bar, directly to where the bartender was standing with his hands out of sight.

"Beer."

"Yeah, sure," the barman said. He pulled his hands from beneath the bar and drew Butler a beer. When he set the mug down in front of him his hands returned to their place under the bar. Butler felt sure the man was caressing a shotgun.

"Where is he?" someone called out. Butler spotted the speaker, standing in a corner.

"Shut up, Toby!" the man at the bar yelled.

Butler marked Toby down as one of the young pups Bat was talking about, did the same for the one at the bar.

It was so quiet in the saloon they all heard Bat's footsteps on the boardwalk. As the lawman entered, the tension heightened. Butler put his beer mug down to keep his hand free. He also tried to signal the bartender with his eyes, but didn't know if his message came across.

"Oh, shit," Bat said. "It's you, Fred."

"It's me, Masterson," the man named Fred said. It was the fella who had told Butler to stay out of trouble. "What's on your mind?"

"I think the question is, what's on yours, Fred."

Butler saw Bat's eyes sweeping the room. He's picking them out, he thought. One by one. So far Butler only had two identified, but Bat would know better since he'd dealt with them before. That meant Butler was going to do better concentrating on his two.

"We're just havin' a good time here, Masterson. No need for the law to interfere."

"Well, you see it as interference, Fred," Bat said, "I

see it as doing my job." Bat leaned over a bit to peer at Tom Reed. "What happened to your mouth, Tom?"

"This young whelp backhanded me, Bat," Reed said. "He didn't have five guns behind him I woulda—"

"Shut up, Tom!"

"Five more guns, eh?" Bat asked. He looked around the room. "Smart man, Fred. You got your men blending in with the crowd, huh?"

Vance said nothing.

"Of course you know that anyone who's not with you is gonna hit the floor when the shooting starts."

Vance frowned. He hadn't thought of that.

"That means I'll be shooting at whoever's standin'."

"Don't matter," Vance said. "We're six against one."

"You like those odds?"

"I'd bet 'em."

"I tell you what," Bat said. "I ain't even gonna shoot at you, Fred. I'm gonna take out your men."

"And I'm gonna take you out, Masterson."

"Naw, you'll be dead," Bat said. "See, I got my own men in with the crowd. One of them has got his eyes on you right now."

It was all Fred Vance could do not to turn around and look. He did hunch his shoulders, though. Butler pictured a bull's-eye right between those shoulders. He'd back shoot the man without a qualm to keep Bat from getting shot.

"Yer bluffin'," Vance said.

"I've never known you to be a good gambler, Fred," Bat said. "You lose with cards, you lose with dice . . . you wanna lose with your life?"

Vance fumed silently, his face starting to burn.

"And for what? Just to prove somethin' to yourself?

That you're a big man? I'll save you the trouble, son. You're not a big man, and nobody thinks you are."

"They will when I kill you."

"Naw," Bat said, "that ain't gonna happen. You touch your gun, Fred, and you'll be dead."

"I'm tired of talkin' to you, Masterson," Vance said. "You been pushing me around ever since you started wearing that tin star. I'm gonna put a bullet right through it."

Bat knew the time for talking had finally passed. Fred Vance finally had his courage up enough. It remained to be seen how many of his five compadres did, too.

"Well then get to it, son," Bat said. "Get to it."

CHAPTER 12

As Vance went for his gun Butler looked at the bartender and shouted, "Now!"

He knew Bat was counting on him to take care of Vance because, even as he caught the shotgun tossed to him by the barman, he saw Bat turning away from the man.

All around them men were hitting the deck, leaving only Vance and his five partners standing. The odds were against Bat and Butler, but at least two of the men hesitated, and that worked in their favor.

Butler triggered one barrel of the shotgun and blew out Fred Vance's spine before the young man could fire his gun at Bat. Meanwhile, Bat fired twice and dropped to one knee.

Butler turned to see who was standing. The one other man he'd picked out seemed stunned by what was happening, but the man next to him was grabbing for his gun. The gambler did not have time to hesitate, or feel sorry for the confused young man, Toby. He pulled the other trigger and blew both of them apart. As they slid down to the floor bloody bits of them adhered to the wall behind them.

Butler dropped the shotgun and drew his gun, but by then it had gone quiet. He looked around and saw no one else standing. Then one by one, several by several, the patrons of the saloon began to get back to their feet, looking around them.

"Goddamn!" Tom Reed said. "That was something!"

Bat was walking around the room, checking on the young would-be gunmen.

"They're all dead," he said to Butler. He turned to the crowd. "I need some volunteers to carry these bodies out of here."

No one moved until Tom Reed shouted, "Get off your asses and volunteer, ya ungrateful bastards."

Men began to come forward and one of them asked Bat, "Where should we take 'em, Marshal?"

"Not enough room at the undertaker's for all of them," Bat said. He was ejecting spent shells from his gun and reloading live ones as he spoke. "Take 'em to the livery down the street, throw 'em in one stall together. The undertaker can collect them from there."

Suddenly there was a flurry of movement as men began hauling bodies out the batwing doors.

Tom Reed came up to Butler and said, "Thanks for the help."

"I invited him," Bat said.

"And thank you, Marshal," Reed said. "I really thought those maniacs were gonna kill somebody today."

"Thank your bartender, too," Butler said, handing the shotgun back to the man. "He was quick."

"I'm gonna give you a raise, Randy."

"Thanks, Boss."

"Get your customers to help you clean up the blood, Tom," Bat said. "I got to get back to work."

"Sure, Marshal, sure. Thanks again. You, too, mister."

"His name's Butler," Bat said. "He'll be in town for a while, working at the Bonanza."

"Well, I don't really care why you're in town, Mr. Butler, just that you were here tonight."

Butler shook hands with the man, then walked out with Bat. He replaced his own empty shells with live loads as they walked back to the saloon.

"How'd you get that bartender to toss you the shotgun?"

"He had his hands on it the whole time. I just sort of . . . sent him a message with my eyes."

"Sharp man," Bat said. "I'm glad he didn't try to use it himself, though. Might have turned out different."

Butler nodded and holstered his gun.

"Wanna deal some faro?" Bat asked. "I have to talk to the undertaker about the bodies."

"Sure," Butler said. "I'll reopen the table right now."

"Okay," Bat said. "I'll be in a little later on. And listen . . . thanks for back there. I don't think me and the kid could've—oh shit, where's the kid?"

Butler turned.

"We forgot about him. He must still be in the back."

"Why didn't he come in when the shooting started?"

"Guess you're going to have to find out."

"Crap," Bat said. "Lemme go find him. I'll catch up to you later."

"I'll be at your table."

Butler was dealing and winning as Bat Masterson entered the saloon about an hour later.

"Close it up," he said as he came by the table. He continued on to the bar to wait.

Butler closed the table despite the protests of the players and joined Bat at the bar.

"What happened?"

"I found the kid in the back room of the saloon," Bat said, accepting a beer from the bartender.

"What happened to him?"

"He's dead," Bat said. "Caught a stray bullet right in the throat. He never had a chance."

"Jesus." Butler asked the bartender for a beer. "I'm sorry, Bat."

"You know what really gets me?"

"What?"

"I was the only one firing in that direction," Bat said. "Must've been my bullet."

"Well, for one thing," Butler said, "I don't think you missed, and for another thing, I was also firing that way. So don't take it on yourself. Might have been me."

"I never should've pinned a badge on him, as green as he was," Bat lamented.

"He was old enough to know what he was doing."

"Yeah, I know," Bat said, "but that don't make me feel any better." He put his beer on the bar half finished. "I got a bottle of whiskey in my room. I'm gonna turn in. You do what you want."

"All right," Butler said. "See you in the morning."

Bat waved and left the saloon, his shoulders slumped.

The bartender, Roscoe, came over.

"I heard," he said. "Too bad."

"Yeah."

"Dean was a nice kid, but Bat was right," Roscoe said. "He never shoulda been wearin' a badge."

"Maybe not," Butler said, "but Bat can't take that all on himself." He picked up his beer. "I'm going to play some more poker."

Roscoe nodded, picked up Bat's unfinished beer, and wiped down the bar with a rag.

CHAPTER 13

Bat was hung over. He had killed a bottle of whiskey that had been half full, and then tumbled into bed. When he woke his head was pounding. It had been a week and he still felt bad about Dean Collier getting killed. He was standing at the bar drinking strong black coffee when Butler came down from his room.

"'morning, Bat."

Bat grunted. Butler signaled to Roscoe, pointing to the cup in Bat's hand and then to himself. He was still communicating well with bartenders, because moments later he had a cup of coffee in his hand, too.

"Bad night?" he asked Bat.

"Worse mornin'," Bat grumbled.

"Bat, you can't still blame yourself—"

Bat raised his hand and said, "One problem at a time. First I've got to get rid of this headache."

Butler could sympathize. He'd woken up plenty of mornings feeling just like that.

"I'm going to go and get some breakfast," Butler said.

"You go," Bat said, waving. "I can't even think about food right now."

"I'll see you later."

"I won't need you for that table till later tonight," Bat said as he went out the door.

Butler waved that he had heard and kept going.

Butler had been taking afternoon walks around Trinidad the past few days, finally trying to get to know the town. He had been surprised to find out it had a population of almost two thousand. Today he peered in the shops, walked through some of the residential sections, checked on his horse, bought some new shirts, and had his boots shined. He sampled a different restaurant for lunch and found it also to his liking. It looked as if eating well was not going to be a problem.

He had a bath, got dressed, put on one of his new shirts, and went downstairs to play some poker. By this time it was almost four, and the saloon was coming to life.

Leaning against a post in front of his office Bat's head was still pounding, but it was starting to fade. He was just thinking he might be ready to get something to eat when he saw three riders coming down Main Street, all dressed in dust-covered black coats, trousers, and hats. Their horse's heads hung low and when he recognized the taller of the three, he thought he was hallucinating. He also took a moment to think that the last two times someone new had ridden into town—Butler last week, and now today—he happened to be on the street to spot them.

The taller rider saw him about the same time and directed his horse that way. The other two followed.

"Well, I'll be damned," Bat said.

"Hello, Bat," Wyatt Earp said.

"Wyatt," Bat said. Then, "Virg, Doc."

Both of the other men simply nodded their heads and touched the brim of their hats.

"Heard you were marshaling up here," Wyatt said. "Thought it might be a place for us to . . . rest a while."

"Plenty of room," Bat said. He stepped down, approached Wyatt, and stuck his hand out. "Good to see you, Wyatt."

"You, too, Bat." The two men shook hands.

"Livery right down the street. Hotel, too. Get yourself settled and come back over here. We'll go and have somethin' to eat, catch up."

"We'll do it, Bat," Wyatt said. "See you in a spell."

Bat watched them ride off toward the livery, wondered what kind of trouble—if any—was following the Earps and Doc Holliday. He was glad to see his friend Wyatt, but couldn't help wondering if their arrival was signaling a change in the wind.

CHAPTER 14

———◆◉◆———

Wyatt and Virgil decided they'd go to their rooms after checking in to the Fairgate Hotel, the closest to the livery, but Doc Holliday had an urge to play some poker. They discussed it in the lobby first.

"After all that ridin'?" Virgil asked.

"Hey," Doc said, "you relax your way and I'll relax mine."

"Go ahead, Doc," Wyatt said. "I'm gonna get cleaned up and check in with Bat. Virg?"

"I'm gonna lie down," Virgil said. "My arm's killin' me."

"Maybe we should find a doctor in town," Wyatt suggested.

"I'm fine," Virgil said. "It hurts when I get tired. You go see Bat, and Doc you go and play cards. I'll be fine."

Doc, who wasn't as worried about Virgil's well-being as Wyatt was, said, "Fine by me. I could use a whiskey, too. Mind my saddlebags?"

"Sure," Wyatt said, taking them from his friend.

Wyatt and Virgil watched as Doc Holliday walked out the front door of the hotel.

"Don't he ever get tired?" Virgil asked. "I seen him sittin' up at night on the trail."

"Doc figures if he lays down he may never get up," Wyatt said. "He's gotta be exhausted to fall asleep, so he tries to exhaust himself."

"Well, he exhausts me," Virgil said. "Want me to put your saddlebags in your room, along with Doc's?"

"No, I want to wash up before I go see Bat."

"I just need to lie down for about an hour," Virgil said. "You go ahead and eat something' if you want."

"You sure you don't want to see a sawbones?"

"I'm fine, Wyatt," Virgil said. "Don't play mother hen, okay?"

"Fine, Virg," Wyatt said. "Have it your way."

They went up to their respective rooms and Wyatt, after having washed his face and hands, came out and pressed his ear to his brother's door. He couldn't hear anything, so he went down the stairs and headed for Bat's office.

Doc Holliday entered the Bonanza saloon, looked around and spotted the poker game that was in progress. At the moment it was the only game in the room. He walked to the bar and ordered a shot of whiskey.

"That a private game or can anyone buy in?" he asked when the barman brought his drink.

"Open to anyone's the way I understand it," the bartender said.

Doc tossed the drink back and said, "Give me another one. I'll take it with me."

The bartender poured and Doc picked up the glass and walked over to the poker table.

"Mind if I sit in?" he asked.

One man looked up and said, "It's Butler's game. You're gonna hafta ask him."

"Okay," Doc said, "which one's Butler?"

"I am," Butler said, "but it's not my game. Anybody can sit in. Pull up a chair."

"Thanks."

Doc sat down, put his drink down at his elbow, and took out his money. There was already money on the table along with the chips so he assumed that his money would play.

"What's the game?" he asked.

"Dealer's choice," Butler said.

"Suits me, I guess."

"What is usually your game, sir?" Butler asked.

"Five-card stud is a preference," Doc said, "but I'll play anything. Butler your only name?"

"Tyrone's my first name," Butler said, "but I usually answer to Butler. And yours?"

"Holliday," he said, "John Holliday."

"Holliday?" This came from Andy Jason, the first man who had spoken. "Like in . . . Doc Holliday?"

"That's what some folks call me," Doc said.

"Go on," a young man standing within earshot said. "You ain't."

Doc turned his head to look at the boy, who had large jug-handle ears and was holding a mug of beer.

"I'm afraid I am, boy."

"Well. I'll be damned," the boy said.

"'Fraid, so will I be, boy," Doc added. "So who's dealin'?"

Butler tried not to look too impressed with Doc Holliday. After all, he already knew Bat Masterson and he had played poker with the likes of Ben Thompson, but Holliday . . . well, he had a reputation as just about as cold a killer as you could get.

He was a slight man, though, slender and not tall, with small hands and blond hair falling from beneath his hat. Not at all what you would have expected of Doc Holliday.

After he misread a couple of hands because he was watching Doc, Butler decided to get his head back into the game. He took the next two hands in a row and got himself back on track.

"Where's Virgil?" Bat asked as Wyatt entered the marshal's office.

"He's restin'," Wyatt said. "Ridin' the trail takes a lot out of him since he got shot."

"I heard about that," Bat said, "and I'm sorry about Morg. I wish I'd been there to help."

"Sounds like you had your hands full in Dodge," Wyatt said. "At least you managed to keep your brother from getting shot."

"You ain't sayin' that Morg and Virg getting shot was your fault, are you?" Bat asked.

"Relocatin' to Tombstone was my idea."

"They coulda said no."

"I s'pose. You got anyplace around here to get a good steak?" Wyatt Earp was obviously uncomfortable talking about his family matters. Bat decided he had to respect that.

"Yeah, we can get you a good steak," Bat said. "Come on, we got a lot of catchin' up to do."

As they stepped outside Bat asked. "Where's Doc?"

"He went to play poker."

"Where?"

"I don't know," Wyatt said. "You got saloons, don't ya? With poker games in 'em? He probably found one of those."

Bat couldn't help wondering if Doc Holliday had found his way to the Bonanza, and Butler's poker game?

"Is there a problem?" Wyatt asked.

"No," Bat said, "there's no problem."

"Good," Wyatt said, "because I'm just about hungry enough to chew off your leg."

CHAPTER 15

After just a few hands Butler was impressed with Doc Holliday's play. He appeared unflappable at the table but he would later find out that this was simply Doc's total disregard for everything. The man didn't care whether he won or lost, he was just marking time. He kept a kerchief handy and coughed into it every so often, coughs that became fits and made other players and people around him uncomfortable. He would come out of one with his face pale and his eyes watery and he'd say, "Excuse me," and people would look away. He would then continue on and play steady, almost deadly poker.

Most people had things eating at them from the inside, but with Doc it was literally eating him away.

On Doc's part, he found Butler to be almost unreadable. He liked that, because he prided himself on being able to read other players. They cared more than he did and it usually showed in their faces and demeanor. It was almost as if Butler had some of the same qualities that he did. There may not have been a disease ravaging his insides, causing him to spit up blood and little bits of his lungs, but there was something going on inside the man.

Tyrone Butler was interesting to Doc. The only other
man he'd ever found remotely interesting was his only
friend, Wyatt Earp.

Bat and Wyatt sat with huge platters of steak and potatoes in front of them. It was still a little early in the day
for Bat to have a meal that big, but Wyatt had been on
the trail eating beans and drinking trail coffee for so long
he wanted to treat him to something special. They were
in a restaurant called D'Amico's, run by an Italian im-
migrant who had somehow found his way to Trinidad.

Wyatt didn't want to talk about what had happened
in Tombstone after Bat left. He also didn't want to talk
about the aftermath, the hunting down of as many of
the cowboys as he and Doc could find. The death of
Johnny Ringo, found lying against the base of a tree,
was still a mystery to most. Bat had read about it in the
newspapers. It was unknown if Ringo had been gunned
by Wyatt, Doc, or perhaps someone else he had fallen
out with.

He did want to talk about Doc Holliday, though.

"Doc is gonna be in trouble if they manage to extradite him back to Arizona," Wyatt said. "And all because
he sided with me."

"So keep him out of Arizona."

"That'll be hard if they come after him with warrants," Wyatt said.

"What about you and Virgil?" Bat asked. "Any warrants out for you?"

"There might be, but I ain't worried about that. We
were wearin' badges when everything happened. Doc
was not even a deputy, he just stood with us. He's got
enough problems of his own without taking on mine,
but he did it."

"Sounds like a good friend," Bat said. Personally, he saw nothing loyal or good about Doc Holliday, but he didn't have to. He was friends with Wyatt, and if Wyatt saw it, it must have been there . . . somewhere.

"What are you gonna do?" he asked.

"Well . . . I was hopin' there was somethin' you could do," Wyatt said, shifting uncomfortably in his seat.

"Like what?"

"Well, I don't like to ask . . ."

"Wyatt, we're friends. Go ahead and ask."

"Well, you're the one wearin' the badge now," Wyatt said. "If you swore out a warrant on Doc, a Colorado warrant, it would—what's the word?—*supersede* an Arizona warrant, wouldn't it?"

"I suppose so, since Doc is here in Colorado."

"And then, if you simply never executed that warrant . . ."

"I see what you're sayin'," Bat replied.

"You'd need to get a judge to swear out the warrant, a judge who didn't much care whether you executed it or not."

"I'm sure I could come up with somebody like that," Bat said, rubbing his jaw.

"Then you'd do it?"

"Not only would I do it," Bat said, "but I will. Just let me give it some thought, figure out how to go about it. You and Doc and Virg can stay here a while."

"Doc's been talkin' about goin' to Denver."

"That probably wouldn't be a problem, since he'd still be in Colorado."

"Bat, I know you and Doc don't see eye to eye," Wyatt said. "This is really decent of you—"

"I'm doin' it for you, Wyatt, not Doc," Bat said. "That shouldn't matter to you, though, as long as it gets done."

"No, you're right," Wyatt said. "Still, I'm grateful."

"Now that we got that cleared up, maybe we can give all of our attention to these steaks?"

Wyatt smiled and said, "Exactly what I was thinkin'."

CHAPTER 16

"I'm out," the third player at the table said. He got up and trudged out of the Bonanza saloon. That left only Butler and Doc Holliday at the table. Between them they had most of the money taken from the other players who had come in and out of the game.

"Head-to-head?" Doc asked.

"No point, really," Butler said. "Seems we're evenly matched, and that kind of game could go on for days."

"Drink at the bar, then?"

"That sounds good."

The two men collected their winnings in paper money and chips. Before moving to the bar they cashed in the chips and stowed their money away in their pockets.

Word had gotten around the saloon that Doc Holliday was there. Butler noticed that he and Doc were given a wide berth as they moved to the bar. Doc did not seem to notice, or simply didn't care.

At the bar Butler got a beer and Doc Holliday a whiskey.

"First round's on me," Doc said. "You get the second."

"You're on."

"Where you from? I haven't heard of you before."

"Back east."

Doc grinned.

"That all you wanna say?"

"That's all that matters," Butler replied.

"As you wish," Doc said, and drained his glass. Butler wasn't finished with his beer yet, but signaled Roscoe to refill Doc's drink.

"How long have you been in Trinidad?"

"A week," Butler said.

"Then you can tell me if it's worth a gambler's time," Doc said. "I was thinkin' of movin' on pretty soon to Denver."

"Can't compare with Denver, I'm sure," Butler said. "If faro's your game— "

"It has been."

"—Bat Masterson's got a table in here."

"Masterson," Doc said. "You met him yet?"

"I have," Butler said. "I knew his brother Jim in Dodge."

"Were you part of that?"

"I was."

"Heard it was some dust-up."

"Probably couldn't compare with what happened in Tombstone, but lead was flying pretty good."

Doc finished his drink, waved at the bartender for a third, and regarded Butler with interest.

"So you're a little more than a gambler."

"I could say the same for you."

Doc lifted his glass.

"Let's drink to variety."

Butler raised his glass.

* * *

As they finished their meal Bat talked about Dodge City and what had occurred there. Wyatt had never asked Bat what had transpired between him and his brother Jim to drive a wedge between them, but he admired his friend for going to his brother's aid anyway.

Bat told Wyatt that he, too, needed someplace to hole up for a while, do some thinking, explained how he had ended up in Trinidad just when the marshal's job was open.

"A man's gotta work," he said, and added that he had the faro layout in the Bonanza.

Then he told Wyatt about the new man who had arrived in town only last week. He also explained the situation where he had pressed Butler's gun into service, and how his deputy had been killed.

"Can't blame yourself for that, Bat," Wyatt said.

"That's what folks have been tellin' me," he said.

"What else do you know about this fella Butler?"

"I know he stood with me, Jim, and Neal Brown in Dodge. Also he was there before I was, already takin' a hand in Jim's troubles. And now he's stepped into mine without so much as a question."

"Sounds a lot like Doc."

"Well, he's a gambler, poker mostly, but I got him relieving me at my faro table in the evenings so I can do my rounds."

"And he's only been here a week?"

"Yeah," Bat said. "Seems he ain't shy about helpin' out."

"Well," Wyatt said, raising his beer glass, "let's drink to friends, then—both old and new."

"That's somethin' I can drink to."

* * *

Virgil Earp woke over an hour later, feeling refreshed despite some dull pain in his arm. But it was the growling in his belly that was the most insistent. He washed his face, strapped on his gun—awkwardly, since he essentially had one good arm—and went downstairs to see if he could find Wyatt. Failing that, he'd just go in search of a decent steak.

The neatest saloon to the hotel was the Bonanza, so he walked over and peered in over the batwing doors. He saw Doc Holliday talking to a man dressed in gambler's black. Seemed the man had already made himself a new friend.

That suited Virgil just fine. He'd never been in favor of his brother's friendship with Doc, even though the man had been invaluable to them during the trouble in Tombstone. Standing with a man in a fight was one thing, but having him for a friend was another.

Virgil moved on.

CHAPTER 17

Virgil spotted Bat and Wyatt coming out of a restaurant. He crossed the street and caught them still talking outside of it.

"You look well fed," he said to Wyatt.

"Good steaks inside, Virg," Wyatt said. "Grab yourself one."

"I will."

"You seen Doc?"

"Yeah," Virgil said, "I just passed the Bonanza saloon. Looks like he found himself a new friend."

As Virgil went inside Wyatt looked at Bat and asked, "Ya think?"

"It wouldn't surprise me if those two found each other," Bat said. "As far as them becoming friends, though, they got a lot in common, but Butler is nothing like Doc when it comes to—" He stopped short.

"Comes to what?" Wyatt asked. "Say it. 'Killin'?"

"I'm just sayin' they're different inside," Bat said. "That's all. And Butler's from the East, he ain't been out here that long."

"Then maybe there's time," Wyatt said.

"Time for what?"

"For him to end up just like Doc."

Bat and Wyatt walked over to the Bonanza and found Butler and Doc right where Virgil said they were, at the bar.

"Didn't take long," Wyatt said. "You found the other gambler in town."

"Plays a pretty mean game of poker, too," Doc said. "Wyatt, this here's Tyrone Butler."

"Mr. Butler," Wyatt said, shaking hands. "Seems we have some friends in common."

"It would seem so," Butler said, "and it's my honor to be counted among them as friends."

"Oh-ho," Wyatt said, looking at Bat, "and he's a smooth talker."

"He's an educated man, Wyatt," Doc said, slurring his words a bit. Butler didn't know how much whiskey Doc had drunk, but that was because he'd lost count.

"Doc," Wyatt said, "how'd you do at the table?"

"Me and this young man cleaned up," Doc said. "Drove them other fellas right outta here."

Doc started to cough then, a fit that sent him staggering. Wyatt was the only one who reached out to steady him. The fit left him looking like death warmed over.

"Time for some rest, Doc?" Wyatt asked. "I know I could use some." Fact was Wyatt didn't feel much like lying down, not with his stomach so full, but he was trying to give his friend a way to withdraw gracefully.

"You might be right, my friend."

"We'll go back to our hotel and see you fellas later," Wyatt said. "I might want to try Mr. Butler out myself, but on the faro table." Wyatt Earp had had a faro layout of his own most everywhere he went.

Butler and Bat watched as Wyatt virtually walked Doc Holliday out of the saloon, but without actually touching him. He was simply there to support his friend if the need arrived.

"I don't know too many people Doc Holliday likes," Bat said to Butler, "and that includes me. You must've impressed him."

"I took some of his money, but he took some of mine," Butler said. "What are they doing in town?"

"Lookin' for a place to lay low for a while," Bat said. "Virgil is with them, too. They been through a lot, especially Wyatt. He blames himself for Virg and Morg's getting shot."

"I think we all know about that kind of guilt, don't we?"

"I do," Bat said. "I don't know about you. Listen, you wouldn't reconsider wearing a deputy's badge while you're here, would ya?"

"I don't think so, Bat," Butler said. "Why don't you ask Wyatt?"

"That wouldn't exactly be layin' low, now would it?"

"No."

"Besides," Bat said, "I'm thinkin' I might be needin' a good hand with a gun as my deputy, because Wyatt, Virg, and Doc are here."

"Well," Butler said, "I'll be around to help, but I don't know that I'd want to go up against any of the three of them with a gun."

"It won't come to that," Bat said. "I'm just worried they might attract some unwanted attention. I mean, I know what that's like myself, so with the four of us here in town it could get worse."

"Like I said," Butler reiterated. "I'll be around."

"I guess that will have to do."

"How are you feeling?" Butler asked.

"Better," Bat said. "I was lucky the bottle wasn't full."

"Well, at least you have something else to occupy your time now," Butler said. "Keeping your friends out of trouble."

"Friend."

"Excuse me?"

"Friend," Bat said, again. "Wyatt's my friend. Doc is his friend, and Virg is Wyatt's brother, but they're not my friends."

"You're just all connected through Wyatt."

"It's complicated," Bat said. "And Wyatt has made it even more complicated."

"How?"

"Come to my office with me and have some coffee," Bat invited, "and I'll tell you."

CHAPTER 18

"You did what?" Virgil asked.

They were having coffee in D'Amico's. Wyatt had gone back after leaving Bat and Butler in the Bonanza, and after taking Doc to his hotel room. Once he was sure his friend was asleep he went to find his brother. They were having coffee together after Virgil's meal.

"I asked Bat to help Doc by swearin' out a warrant for his arrest."

"In Colorado."

"Yes."

"You think that will keep Arizona from getting him back?"

"I hope so."

Virgil shook his head, cut into his pie.

"You're a good friend, Wyatt," he said. "I wish I had a friend like you."

"You do, Virg," Wyatt said. "Only I happen to be your brother, too."

"Yeah, well," Virgil said, "what're we gonna be doin' while Doc's hidin' out in Colorado?"

"I'm not done, yet," Wyatt said. "There's a place here in Colorado called Glenwood Springs. There's a sanitarium there where people like Doc can get some help."

"What kind of help."

"With his lungs," Wyatt said. "It has something to do with the sulfur springs there, supposed to be good for people like Doc."

"People who are dying, you mean?" Virgil asked.

Wyatt sat back.

"Maybe not," he said. "Maybe there's time to reverse it."

"Come on, Wyatt," Virgil said. "Every time he has one of those coughing fits little flecks of his lungs come up with the blood. He's gonna die and there's nothin' you can do about it. My God, even he knows that."

Virgil rubbed his left arm, grimacing.

"Are you in pain?" Wyatt asked.

"All the time, little brother."

"Come on." Wyatt pushed his chair back and got to his feet.

"Where to?"

"We're gonna find the sawbones in this town."

"Wyatt—"

"Maybe he can't fix your arm but he sure as hell can give you somethin' for the pain."

"You mean like laudanum?" Virgil asked. "The stuff Mattie was on? I don't want to be doped up all the time, Wyatt."

The reference to Wyatt's second wife brought him back into his seat. In his mind he had already moved on from Mattie to Josie, even though he was still married to her.

"I'm sorry, Virg, I just—"

"Look, when I get to Denver I'll see a good doctor there."

"You goin' to Denver?"

"I was thinkin' about it."

"That's where Doc wants to go."

"I know. He wants to gamble, though."

"And you?"

Virgil shrugged.

"They got good doctors there."

"So you have been thinkin' about it."

Virgil touched his arm again.

"Believe me, Wyatt," he said, "I think about this all the time."

"So he wants to phony up a warrant?" Butler asked later. "Make a bogus arrest?"

"No arrest," Bat said, "just a phony warrant."

"For Doc."

"Right."

"Who's not your friend."

"But Wyatt is, and he's doin' the askin'."

"You're right."

"About what?"

"It is complicated."

Butler got up, walked over to the potbellied stove and poured himself another cup of Bat's coffee, which was remarkably good. As he did he noticed a deputy's badge sitting on the stove next to the coffeepot. The metal was undoubtedly hot and he wondered what kind of symbolism was in that fact? Whatever it was it was too deep for him. Interpreting that was for better educated people than he. He left the badge there—where Bat had obviously put it—and didn't mention it.

He turned and went back to his seat across from the marshal.

"So what are you going to do?"

"I'm gonna do my friend a favor," Bat answered, "and try to keep his friend from being arrested."

"Do you know a judge who will go along with you on this?"

Bat seemed to be concentrating, sitting back in his seat with his chin almost on his chest. "I think I do."

"What kind of trouble could this get you into?"

"I don't know," Bat said. "I've never done this before."

"Will Doc have to stay here, in Trinidad?"

"No, but he'll have to stay in Colorado—or, at least, stay out of Arizona." Bat thought a moment. "No, he'll have to stay in Colorado."

"Think he'll do that?"

"There's no predicting what Doc Holliday will or will not do," Bat said. "I can only do this favor for Wyatt and see how it turns out."

"Well," Butler said, "I only hope you can do it without causing yourself too much trouble."

"If there's trouble I'll deal with it then," Bat said. "That's the way I've always done it. No point in worryin' about somethin' before it happens."

"Good philosophy," Butler said.

"It's not philosophy," Bat said. "It's just a rule."

CHAPTER 19

———◆◉◆———

Late that night Butler was manning Bat's table while the lawman did his rounds. He had less time for the table now that he had no deputy. Butler was taking money from all comers when the batwing doors swung inward and both Wyatt and Virgil Earp entered.

Word had gotten around that not only was Doc Holliday in town, but the Earps, so they drew looks as they entered and approached the bar. Wyatt looked over at Butler and exchanged a nod with him. The two ex-lawmen then ordered beers and stood at the bar drinking them. Butler wondered if and when Wyatt was going to come over and try him. He didn't anticipate that he'd have much luck against the man. He was a much stronger poker player than a faro dealer, and faro was Wyatt Earp's game.

He was still waiting when Bat Masterson walked in, looked around, nodded to him, and then joined the Earps at the bar. Now he wondered where Doc Holliday was, and if he was all right. He hadn't looked all that good that afternoon when Wyatt Earp walked him out of the Bonanza.

Finally, Bat tore himself away from the Earps and ambled over to Butler and the faro table. At that moment there were no takers.

"Looks like you've scared all the players away," Bat said. "Might as well close up. I don't feel like dealin' tonight, and you might still get into a poker game."

"Mind if I just join you at the bar?" Butler asked.

"Be my guest."

Together they covered the table and then walked over to the bar, where the Earps each had a fresh beer.

"Drinks on me, Butler," Wyatt said. "What'll you have?"

"Beer," Butler told Willy, the young bartender.

"Looks like you were doin' pretty good tonight," Wyatt commented as Butler accepted his beer.

"Not bad," Butler said. "I thought you were going to come over and try your luck."

"I don't mind tryin' my luck," Wyatt said, "I just didn't want to try yours, tonight."

"The cards were running well for me," Butler admitted. He just as soon not face Wyatt Earp across the faro table. So he figured he'd dodged the bullet tonight.

"Where's Doc tonight?"

"Still restin', I hope," Wyatt said. "That was a pretty bad episode he had this afternoon."

"Did you talk to him yet about this warrant business?" Bat asked Wyatt.

"No," Wyatt said. "I thought I'd wait until tonight."

"Why would he have anythin' bad to say about it?" Virgil asked. "It's gonna help him out."

"You never know how Doc's gonna react to somethin'," Wyatt said. "Even something that's supposed to help him."

"You talk to him about Glenwood Springs yet?" Virgil asked.

"Glenwood Springs?" Bat asked. "Ain't that where they got those, uh, sulfer springs?"

"That's the place," Wyatt said.

"That should be good for him," Butler added.

"If I can get him to go," Wyatt said. "Doc's pretty stubborn."

"Too stubborn to want to live?" Butler asked.

"Doc wants to live, but he wants to live his way," Wyatt said, "on his own terms. Nobody can tell him different."

"Maybe you can, Wyatt," Virgil said. "He listens to you."

"Maybe," Wyatt said.

"You can start working on him right now," Butler said, his eyes on the front door, where Doc Holliday had just entered.

Patrons in the Bonanza began to get restless. Here were three of the principals in the event that had already become known as the Shootout at the O.K.Corral, all in one room together, along with Bat Masterson. In addition, word had gotten around that Bat and Butler had shot up the Bucket of Blood the night before, killing three men.

"Looks like you might start losing some customers," Butler said.

"The hell with 'em," Bat said. "Willy, get me a beer, will you?"

"Sure, Marshal."

"What'll ya have, Doc?" Bat asked.

"Whiskey," Doc said, his voice sounding hoarse. He tried to clear his throat and almost went into another coughing fit, but was able to quell it.

Willy poured the whiskey and his hand shook. Of all the men standing at the bar it was Doc Holliday he was most in awe of. The others, although they had reputations with their guns, were also gamblers and lawmen. Doc's reputation was that of a killer, pure and simple.

"Relax, kid," Doc said, accepting the glass. "I'm not going to bite you."

"Y-yes, sir," Willy said. "I mean, no, sir."

Doc turned to face the others with his drink in hand.

"No faro tonight?" he asked.

"Closed the table," Bat said. "Butler was cleanin' everybody out."

Doc looked over at the batwings, which were swinging in and out quickly as people filed out.

"Am I costin' you business?" he asked.

"Don't worry about them," Bat said. "Let's get a table now that the place has cleared out.

The five of them picked up their drinks and moved to a back table. Three men sitting at a table nearby picked up their drinks and moved away. Butler didn't know what their problem was. He felt as if he was in pretty august company.

They had their drinks while Bat and Wyatt exchanged some small talk and then Doc said, "Okay, what's goin'on?"

"Whataya mean, Doc?"

"Somethin's on your mind," Doc said. "All of you. I can feel it ever since I came in."

The four men looked at one another, each waiting for someone else to talk. Butler sat back, because he was the outsider. He had nothing to say.

"Come on," Doc said, "somebody better start talkin'."

Virgil looked at his brother and said, "Wyatt?"

Wyatt gave his brother a dirty look, then said to his friend, "Okay, Doc, here it is . . ."

CHAPTER 20

————◆————

"Isn't a sanitarium a place where they send crazy people?" Doc asked when Wyatt finished his pitch.

"No," Wyatt said, "it's for sick people, Doc. People who are . . . well, like you. I mean, not like you but who have—"

"Okay, Wyatt," Doc said, raising his hand, "I know what you mean." Butler had noticed the night before how long and tapered Doc's fingers seemed to be. Also, how skinny his wrists were. "I get it."

"What do you think, Doc?" Wyatt said.

"I'll give it some thought," Doc said. "Right now I'm going to get another drink. Anyone else want one?"

They were all drinking beer and had plenty left.

"He took it well," Virgil said.

"I thought he took it well," Butler said. "Except for that part about the crazy people."

"He's not gonna go," Wyatt said.

"Well," Bat said, "when he comes back maybe we should talk about the warrants."

"Yeah," Wyatt said, "he might take that a little easier."

They all fell quiet as Doc returned with his fresh drink. He sat and looked around at them.

"That isn't it, is it?" he asked. "There's more?"

"This is different," Wyatt said. "You know there are warrants out for your arrest in Arizona."

"There's warrants on all of us," Doc pointed out.

"Yeah, but Virg and I were wearin' badges," Wyatt said. "We can work that out. You didn't have a badge, Doc, so you're at risk to be extradited back to Arizona, and tried."

"And you got a solution?"

"I think so," Wyatt said. "Bat's gonna arrest you."

"What?"

"Well, not really arrest you," Wyatt said quickly. "He's gonna have a judge swear out a warrant against you. With an active warrant in Colorado, they won't be able to drag you back to Tombstone to stand trial."

Doc looked to be mulling this over, then looked at Bat.

"You can do that?"

"I have to talk to this judge I know," Bat said, "but I think I can swing it, yeah."

"So there'd be a warrant out for my arrest, but no one in Colorado would act on it."

"Right."

Doc toyed with his glass for a few seconds, then asked Bat, "Why would you do this?"

"Truthfully? Because Wyatt asked me to."

Doc looked at Wyatt, who shrugged.

"Good enough for me," Doc said. "I, uh, am much obliged, Bat."

"Sure," Bat said. "No guarantee, but I should know somethin' in a few days. Can you stay that long?"

Doc and Wyatt exchanged a glance and then Doc said, "I don't see why not."

"I'm gonna move on, if nobody minds," Virgil said.

"Wyatt, you might as well go with him," Doc said. "I'll be fine here for a few days, until Bat figures this out."

"Where you headin', Virg?" Bat asked.

"Denver, I think. After that, I ain't sure."

"Denver's good enough for me," Wyatt said. "After that I think I'll join Josie in California."

Doc looked at Bat this time and said, "Might be I'll be keepin' some of your customers away. I could do my drinkin' and gamblin' in another saloon in town, if you like."

"Naw," Bat said. "Once folks get used to you bein' around they'll probably come in here just to have a look. So I guess it's up to you whether or not you wanna be gawked at."

"You stayin' around awhile, Butler?" Doc asked.

Butler shrugged, said, "I'm not in a hurry to go anywhere. Like Wyatt I'll be heading for California soon enough, but not for a while."

"Where in California?" Wyatt asked.

"I thought I'd do some gambling in San Francisco."

"Portsmouth Square?"

"Yes," Butler said. "I heard the gambling houses there are amazing."

"They are," Wyatt said. "Luke Short's been there quite a bit."

"Been there myself," Bat said. "It's somethin' to see, all right, and you'll see some of the big names there, like Luke."

"Dick Clark," Wyatt said.

"Poker Alice," Bat added.

"Ben Thompson," Doc Holliday said.

"I played with Ben Thompson," Butler said. "Pretty damn good poker player."

"Best hand with a gun I ever saw," Bat said grudgingly.

"That a fact?" Doc Holliday asked.

"So far," Bat said.

"Speaking of poker," Virgil said, "anybody game? I got nothin' to do for a while."

They all looked at one another and then Bat said, "I'll go get a deck and some chips."

CHAPTER 21

Wyatt Earp, Virgil Earp, Doc Holliday, Bat Masterson, and Ty Butler sitting at the same table playing poker attracted some attention. Little by little men began to come into the saloon—or back into the saloon—to watch. It didn't seem to matter that the stakes were low, people just wanted to see who was going to come out on top.

It was Virgil's idea, so he set the rules. They all started with two hundred dollars and there were no rebuys. When you lost your stake you were out, and it was a winner-take-all competition. They all agreed.

First out was Virgil who, despite the fact that the game was his idea, was not truly a gambler. Not in the sense the others were.

"Just as well," he announced, standing up. "My arm's startin' to hurt. I'm gonna see if I can get some sleep."

He staggered a bit as he left the table. He'd been drinking whiskey for the past hour in the hopes of dulling the pain.

"Virg, you want me to walk you—"

"Naw, I'll be fine, Wyatt," his brother said. "You stay and take these fellas' money. We can use it in Denver."

Wyatt kept a wary eye on his brother until he was out the door. Suddenly, unbidden, came the memory of Morgan lying on top of a pool table while they tried to stop the bleeding from his mortal wound. Though Morg was ambushed that night, there was no reason to believe anyone in Trinidad would try to ambush Virgil.

"Why don't you follow him?" Bat asked.

"No," Wyatt said, "he'll snap at me for bein' a mother hen. Just deal the damn cards."

Faro was Wyatt's game, so he wasn't embarrassed or annoyed when Butler bluffed him out of a hand and broke him about half an hour later.

"Well, at least I can go and check on Virg," he said, standing up. "See you gents in the mornin'. Take their money, Doc."

"Will do."

Wyatt left, walking straight as an arrow because he had not had more than a second beer.

"Well," Bat said, "I guess it's just the three of us."

He dealt the cards. They were playing five-card stud. The game had started out as dealer's choice, but gradually they all began to deal five stud each time.

He dealt one down, one up. Doc got a king of spades, Butler an eight of hearts, and Bat a Jack of clubs.

"King bets."

"Twenty," Doc said.

The money left behind by the Earps was pretty evenly distributed among the three men.

"Call," Butler said.

"My jack raises," Bat said. "Another twenty."

"Call," Doc said.

"I call."

Both Bat and Doc looked at Butler's eight of hearts.

"Comin' out," Bat said. He dealt out their third card. Doc got another king, Butler a six of hearts, and Bat another jack.

"Kings bet."

"I'll bet into the raiser with my kings," Doc announced. "Fifty."

"I call," Butler said.

"Raise," Bat said, "another fifty."

"Call," Doc said.

"I call," Butler said.

Doc and Bat looked at him, and his six and eight of hearts.

"What, I can't call?"

"With that hand?" Doc asked.

"Three-card straight at best," Bat said.

"Or a three-card flush."

"Yup."

"Why don't you fellas pay attention to your own hands?" Butler asked.

"Okay," Bat said, "here we go."

He dealt them each their fourth card.

Doc's kings did not improve with the addition of a three of diamonds.

Butler caught a five of hearts.

Bat didn't improve on his jacks, either, when a four of clubs fell.

"Kings bet," Bat said.

"I'll check to the raiser," Doc said.

"I'm feeling lucky," Butler said. "I'll bet a hundred."

"What the—" Bat said. "I raise a hundred. You just bluffed Wyatt out and now you're tryin' it with us."

Doc stared at Butler for a few moments, then said, "He ain't bluffin'. He ain't got nothin' yet, but he ain't bluffin', either. He's really bettin' his luck, bettin' on the come."

"I can see callin' on the come," Bat said, "but not raisin'. Whataya do, Doc?"

"I'm gonna call."

"Last card," Bat said, and dealt it out. He and Doc did not improve. Butler's card busted his straight or flush, but paired his sixes.

"Kings bet," Bat said. "Doc?"

Doc studied his hole card for a few moments, then studied Bat and Butler in turn.

"Check."

"I bet a hundred," Butler said.

"I raise," Bat said.

"I fold my kings," Doc said. "I believe one of you."

"Which one?" Bat asked.

Doc shrugged.

"In the long run it doesn't matter, does it? One of you has me beat. I fold, I save money."

"I reraise, Bat," Butler said.

Bat looked at Doc, who shrugged, then looked at Butler, who gave him nothing.

"I'm gonna call you, because I wanna see," Bat said. Then he turned over his cards. "Beat two pair, jacks over."

Butler turned over his hole card. It was a six of diamonds, giving him three sixes.

"No bluff," Doc said. "Glad I folded my kings over."

"You had me beat, too?" Bat asked, exasperated.

"Looks like it." Doc turned over his cards to show that he was telling the truth, he had a higher two pair than Bat.

Doc started collecting the cards because he had the next deal.

"Nice hand, Butler," Bat said.

"Thanks, Bat."

"I'll get you next time."

"The next time is now," Doc said, shuffling expertly. "Comin' out. Five-card stud again, gents."

"I wouldn't have it any other way."

CHAPTER 22

The game went on for hours and the three of them finally had to call it a night. The money was pretty evenly split, and Bat offered each of them a final drink before he closed the Bonanza doors.

"Well," Doc said, over his last whiskey, "that didn't prove much, did it?"

"It proved that Virgil's no card player, and Wyatt should stick to faro," Bat said.

Butler looked around. Except for Roscoe, the bartender, they were alone in the place. Doc was the only one who had to leave the building to walk to his hotel, while Butler and Bat both had rooms upstairs.

Something didn't feel right to Butler. He looked around again. This time he thought he saw a shadow at the front window.

"Guess I better turn in," Doc said. He'd been drinking whiskey during the game and his eyes were bloodshot. His coughing fits had been kept to a minimum. Butler wondered if the whiskey actually helped with that.

Butler put his hand on Bat's arm.

"Something's not right."

"I know," Bat said. "You walk him, I'll go out the back."

"Right."

All three of them walked to the front door, where Butler said, "I need some air. I'm going to walk to the hotel with you, Doc."

"Suit yourself," Doc said. Suddenly, it was as if he could not keep his eyes open. Butler wondered if the man would have even made it to the hotel if he hadn't decided to walk him.

Bat said good night and locked the doors behind them.

Trinidad's streets had lamps to light the way, but, at the same time, lamps would cast shadows—shadows deep enough for a man to hide in.

"You felt it, too?" Doc asked as they walked.

"Yes," Butler said. "Something . . ."

"You or me?" Doc asked.

"I guess it could be me," Butler said, "but I didn't really have to leave the building."

"Me, then."

"Tonight, anyway."

"You got somebody on your trail?" Doc asked.

"You never know."

"It's a helluva way to live, ain't it?"

"It'd be a hell of a way to die, too."

They walked slowly, keeping to the boardwalk and out of the street, until they reached Doc's hotel.

"Were we wrong?" Butler asked.

"No," Doc said. "There were two of us. Whoever's out there wasn't prepared for that."

"Bat's out there," Butler said.

"Maybe he'll find them," Doc said. He coughed, covered his mouth with a kerchief, but nothing came up. "Okay, so you walked me back, now how about you?"

"Like I said," Butler repeated, "Bat's out there."

"Still . . ."

"Go on, Doc," Butler said. "Get some rest. I'll see you tomorrow."

Doc lingered, then said, "All right. Good night."

"'Night."

Doc went into the hotel, crossed the lobby, and went up the stairs. Butler waited, giving the man enough time to get to his room. When there were no shots from inside the hotel he figured Doc had made it.

Now it was his turn.

Bat had been in the shadows, walking behind Doc and Butler on the same side of the street. He kept his eyes on the other side of the street, though, thinking that if an ambush came it would be from there.

He waited while Butler and Doc talked in front of the hotel, then watched as Doc went inside. Butler started back to the Bonanza, and Bat decided to join him. He came out of the shadows and fell in beside the gambler.

"Somebody changed their mind," he said.

"Doc felt it, too," Butler said. "Somebody in this town has got ideas."

"Well," Bat said, "Wyatt and Virgil are leavin', and Doc is stayin'."

"So am I."

"It's one of you two they're interested in," Bat said. "I guess we'll find out sooner or later."

"I guess we will."

CHAPTER 23

————◆————

Butler came out of the café after breakfast the next morning and encountered Bat Masterson on the street.

"A little late for breakfast for you, isn't it?" he asked.

"Had breakfast," Bat said. "Had it with Wyatt and Virgil. They wanted to get an early start."

"Sorry I didn't get a chance to say good-bye," Butler said. "Still heading for Denver?"

"Yep," Bat said, "they want to get a good doctor to take a look at Virg's arm."

"It'll be a tough thing for him to be a lawman with one arm," Butler observed.

"Yeah, he mentioned that," Bat said. "He was saying he might go private if he can't wear a badge anymore."

"A detective, you mean?"

"Yeah, but that'll come later."

"Where are you headed now?"

"Courthouse," Bat said. "I told Wyatt I'd check into that warrant on Doc and send him a telegram in Denver."

"The judge you're thinking about is in town?"

Bat nodded.

"That's why I thought of him," he said. "He's here for three days. I'm gonna talk to him right now. Wanna come?"

"Don't think I'd be any help," Butler said, "but I'll walk over with you."

As they walked toward the courthouse Bat said, "Wyatt made me promise to look after Doc."

"That's not a job anyone would volunteer for."

"He says Doc's fine in a fight, but it's the other parts of his life where he needs lookin' after."

"Maybe he needs a woman."

"I thought he had one," Bat said. "He and Big Nose Kate were together for a long time."

"What happened?"

"I don't know, and I ain't about to ask," Bat said. "That's one part of a man's life I don't get involved in. What's between him and his woman is between him and his woman, if you get what I mean."

"I get it," Butler said. "Is that something else that's a rule with you, and not a philosophy?"

"Definitely. For me to have a philosophy I'd have to be a helluva lot better educated. Rules are easier."

"Easier to make, maybe," Butler said. "Not necessarily easier to stick to."

"Sounds like you may have broken a few of your own rules along the way," Bat said.

"Shattered, is more like it."

"Well, if you're gonna break a rule," Bat agreed, "you might as well shatter it."

They reached the courthouse, a two-story brick building.

"I won't bother going in with you," Butler said. There was a wooden bench right in front. "I'll sit here and wait, and watch the folks go by."

"Suit yourself," Bat said. "Shouldn't take me long to present my case to Judge Abernathy."

"You been here a matter of months and already you've got a judge beholding to you?"

"You just got to be in the right place at the right time." Bat opened the door to enter, then turned to Butler. "There's a place right down the block if you get a hankerin' for another cup of coffee. Don't eat there, but the coffee's decent."

"I'll remember."

"Doc's not up yet?"

"I don't know," Butler said. "I didn't think to check."

"That's okay," Bat said. "I'm the one supposed to be checkin' up on him. Okay, let me get this over with."

Bat went inside, the door closing loudly behind him. Butler thanked his lucky stars he hadn't been the first one to see Wyatt Earp that morning. He would not have wanted to be saddled with the job of looking out for Doc Holliday—although, that's what he had been doing the night before, walking the man back to his hotel. Still, that had been willingly, and not a responsibility put on him by a friend.

Butler watched as townspeople walked by, stores opened. Men eyed him suspiciously, women looked at him with a mixture of feelings. Could have been anything going through their minds from Who is that man to Why can't my husband dress that nice early in the day.

The street began to fill with traffic, men on horses, men and women riding buckboards or buggies into town to do their shopping. Butler found his mind going back to the deputy's badge sitting on the stove in Bat's office. He wondered if Bat had left it there, if it would melt the longer it sat there. He never once thought about pinning it on, though. He was a gambler, not a lawman. He'd leave mixing those two occupations to the likes of the Mastersons and the Earps.

After about half an hour of watching the town wake up, he began to get restless. He was thinking about going down the street for that extra cup of coffee when the front door opened and Bat came out.

"How did it go?"

"It took some doin'," Bat said, "but I got him to see it my way."

"He'll swear out the warrant?"

Bat nodded. "I should have it later today."

"That's good news for Bat, and a load off of Wyatt's mind once you send him a telegram."

"I'll send that today, too, have it waitin' for him when he gets there. Now, I could use a cup of coffee. Walk down the street with me?"

"I was just thinking the same thing."

CHAPTER 24

Wherever men like Bat Masterson and Doc Holliday were, there were men like Frank Pennington.

Pennington was what was known in the West as a "mudsill." It meant he was worthless, a nobody. It also meant that when he saw someone who had a reputation, he usually felt he was entitled to it.

Bad enough Bat Masterson was the marshal in Trinidad, but now Doc Holliday was there.

In Pennington's mind, even if he had been able to back shoot Masterson or Doc Holliday, it would make him worth something, give him a reputation, even in his own mind.

He'd been in the saloon the night before when they all walked in, the Earps, Doc Holliday, and Masterson. He'd also been among the men who had filed out to look for someplace else to drink, but unlike the others he'd lingered outside in the shadows, waiting. He really didn't care who he caught coming out, but somebody was going to pay for the fact that Frank Pennington was a nobody.

Virgil Earp had come out first. Pennington figured there was no percentage in back shooting a cripple, so he let him go.

Wyatt Earp came out next, but by this time Pennington had convinced himself that he wanted the lunger, Doc Holliday. He figured he'd be putting the poor bastard out of his misery by gunning him down in the street, then he'd do himself good by letting the word slip out that he'd done it. Thirty years on this earth and he hadn't done anything worth a damn, but he figured to change that right quick.

Then when Doc Holliday came out that gambler came with him. Back shooting one man was one thing, but he wasn't about to take two men on at the same time. Especially not after what he'd heard about the gambler and Masterson shooting up the Bucket of Blood.

So Pennington had backed off, and today he was sitting in a small saloon down the street from the Bucket. This was the only saloon in town that opened in the morning, only place a man could get a decent drink this early. He had arranged to meet three men here, because he figured he was going to need a little help if that gambler, Butler, had taken up with Holliday.

His friends were of the same ilk as he, although a couple of them were "waddies," cowpokes working on nearby ranches. Still, in their hearts they were mudsills, like he was.

Around town, unbeknownst to them, they were all simply known as "coffee boilers," men who'd rather shirk their duty and sit around the coffeepot.

His three friends filed in, looking the worse for wear after a hard night at the Bucket of Blood.

Deke Walton, Seth Cates, and Waldo Ferguson filed in, stopped at the bar for a beer, and then joined Pennington at his table.

"What's so important you got to get us up this early?" Waldo complained bitterly.

"Early?" Pennington asked. "You fellas work on a ranch. Ain't you up at the crack of dawn?"

Waldo Ferguson looked over at Deke Walton, who said, "Ah, we got fired yesterday."

"Fired? It's about time. They finally realized what lay-abouts you two are?" Seth Cates said, laughing.

"At least we had jobs," Waldo said.

"Jobs are for suckers," Cates said. "I'll bet Frank's got somethin' hot for us."

"I got somethin'," Pennington said. "It ain't gonna make us no money right away, but it'll give us a name."

"You still singin' that same old song?" Waldo asked. "Gonna make a name for yerself? Why don't you just admit none of us is ever gonna amount to nothin'."

"You ain't never gonna be nothin' with that attitude," Pennington said. "I ain't like that."

"So whataya got, Frank?" Seth asked. Seth Cates was close to being the town drunk, except that honor was usually reserved for older men than he. But he was usually pretty roistered, and ready for any half-baked scheme Frank Pennington could come up with.

"I got Doc Holliday," Pennington said.

"What about him?" Waldo asked.

"He's in town."

"We know that," Deke Walton said. "So are the Earps."

"They pulled out early this mornin'," Pennington said. "Now Holliday is here by himself."

"So?" Waldo still didn't get it.

Seth thought he did.

"We gonna rob 'im, Frank?"

"No," Pennington said. "We ain't gonna rob him. We're gonna kill 'im."

The other three were silent for a few moments, then
Seth asked, "Can't we rob him, too?"

"Kill him?" Waldo asked, ignoring Seth. "What for?
He's a lunger. He's gonna cough himself to death soon,
anyway."

"Not if we get to him first," Pennington said. "Imagine bein' the men who killed Doc Holliday?"

"Yeah," Waldo said, "we'll be the most famous men
in prison."

"We ain't goin' to prison," Pennington said.

"We are if we gun down Doc Holliday," Waldo said.

"Just shut up for a minute and listen," Pennington
said, "and you'll see what I mean."

CHAPTER 25

When Bat and Butler hit the street again Bat said, "I might as well give Doc the word." They had each had a cup of coffee, and then gone together to the telegraph office, where Bat sent a telegram to Denver. He knew Wyatt and Virgil were going to be staying at the Denver House Hotel. The telegram would be waiting for them when they got in.

"I guess he'll be glad he won't have to stay around here for more than a few days."

"Maybe not even that," Bat said. "Judge Abernathy is usually quick. He'll draw it up and have to file it with the state."

"What happens if somebody else in Colorado realizes there's a warrant and decides to execute it?"

"Word'll get back to me or the judge," Bat said.

"And what's the charge?"

"Well, I had to make it somethin' serious enough," Bat said. "It couldn't be for spittin' on the street or somethin'."

"So what is it?"

"I cited him for lewd conduct," Bat said.

"Jesus . . ."

"He'll get a kick out of it."

"You think so?"

"Hey, it'll keep him out of jail for murder."

"I don't know . . ."

"Let's go tell him and see," Bat said.

"Doc Holliday doesn't seem like the kind of man who can take a joke," Butler said, "but let's go."

"I don't like it," Waldo Ferguson said.

"Why not?" Pennington demanded.

"Well, for one thing it ain't like Doc Holliday's here all hisself," Waldo complained. "Masterson's here, and I was in the Bucket of Blood when him and that gambler shot up Fred Vance and his boys slicker'n snot. That gambler—what's his name—Butler? He handles a shotgun about as good as he handles a deck of cards."

Pennington decided not to tell Waldo and the others that it looked like Butler had become friends with Holliday. He'd keep that little bit of information to himself.

"Look," he said, "it ain't like we're gonna face 'im head on."

"Whataya mean?" Seth asked. "We gonna dry gulch 'em?"

"How else you gonna kill somebody like Doc Holliday?" Pennington asked. "Jesus, I ain't stupid enough to stand in front of him."

"I dunno," Waldo said.

"You don't know what?" Pennington asked.

"I just ain't never seen myself as a dry gulcher, Frank."

"Waldo, you ain't never seen yerself as anything," Pennington said. "That's your problem." He looked at the other two. "What about you? You got a problem bushwackin' a dirty killer like Doc Holliday? Hell, we'll be doin' people a favor."

"I don't have no problem with it, Frank," Seth said. "You know me. I'm ready for anythin'."

"Deke?"

"Sure," Deke Walton said, "why not? I sure don't want to go back to punchin' cows."

"That leaves you, Waldo," Pennington said, giving the man a hard look. "You with us, or against us?"

"I ain't against ya, Frank," Waldo said, hurriedly.

"You are if you ain't with us," Pennington said. "Come on, make your play. You gonna make somethin' of yerself or not?"

Waldo Ferguson didn't know if he wanted to make somethin' of himself, but he sure didn't want these three thinkin' he was against them.

"Okay, Frank, okay," he said finally. "I'm with ya. When are we gonna do this thing?"

"That's somethin' we gotta talk about," Pennington said. "When, and where. Let's get some more beers."

"I'll get 'em," Seth said, excitedly, then looked at Pennington and asked, "You got any money, Frank?"

Bat and Butler were prepared to knock on Doc Holliday's door—god forbid he was dead in there, how would Bat explain that to Wyatt Earp—but there was no need to. As they entered the hotel Doc came down the stairs to the lobby. Dressed in black he looked both frail and pale, but at the same time as healthy as they had seen him.

"'Mornin', Doc," Bat said.

"Bat, Butler," Doc said. "You lookin' for me already? Sorry I'm up so late. Wyatt and Virgil get away okay?"

"Early this mornin', Doc," Bat said. "Said to tell you they'll see you on the trail somewhere."

"Yeah, we will," Doc said. "If I last long enough."

"Give any more thought to that Glenwood Springs thing?" Bat asked, making Butler cringe, but there was no need.

"Actually, I have," Doc said. "But there's still time. I can still stand on my feet, anyway. If I decide to go there I'll walk in myself, I won't make anybody carry me."

Neither Bat nor Butler knew what to say to that.

"What're you lookin' for me for?" Doc asked then.

"Got some news about that warrant," Bat said.

"Take some air with me and tell me about it," Doc said, heading for the door.

CHAPTER 26

"You would think that was funny," Doc said to Bat moments later.

"Oh, I can change it if you—"

"No, no," Doc said. "What's it matter? My reputation can't get any worse than it is right now. Let it stand."

"Okay," Bat said. "I'll let you know as soon as I have it in my hand. Shouldn't be more than a couple days."

"That's fine," Doc said. "By then I'll be ready to move on. By then I'll also have some of this young man's money to take with me."

"Oh-ho, that sounds like a challenge," Butler said. "I'll see you in the Bonanza tonight, my friend."

"Bring plenty of money," Doc said. "I've been takin' it easy on you until now."

"This sounds like a game I'm gonna stay out of," Bat said. "I've got some rounds to make, boys. If you'll excuse me."

"See you later, Bat," Butler said.

"Much obliged for the information, Bat," Doc said, "if not the, uh, extra smudge on my rep."

"Glad to be of help, Doc."

Bat left Butler and Doc Holliday there on the board-walk.

"He's a good friend to Wyatt," Doc said.

"Seems to me Wyatt's got a lot of good friends," Butler said. "How does he rate that?"

"He's an honorable man," was all Doc said then, "I'm going to continue on walkin'."

Butler had the feeling Doc wanted to walk by himself and think.

"I've got some things to tend to myself," Butler said. "I'll see you later at the Bonanza."

"I look forward to it."

"We just have to catch Holliday off by himself," Frank Pennington told the others.

"How do we do that?" Waldo asked.

"We watch him."

"When?" Seth asked.

"Startin' now," Pennington said. "Today."

"How do we do that?" Deke asked.

"Well, Jesus," Pennington said, "do I have to tell you everything? We all get out there and look for him. Whoever finds him will have to find the others."

"How do we—"

"We go out in twos," Pennington said. "Seth, you're with me. Waldo and Deke, you go south of town, Seth and I will go north."

"Why don't we just start at his hotel?" Seth asked as the other two left.

"At this time of the mornin' he's bound to already be up and around," Pennington said. "Come on, we got things to do."

"Hey," Seth said, "if we find him first, we can just take him. Why do we need Waldo and Deke?"

"We'll see," Pennington said. "Let's just decide that when the time comes, okay?"

Butler spent the afternoon checking on his horse, cleaning his guns, looking at some new boots, and then going back to the Bonanza to make sure there were new decks for the game that night. He didn't know how many men would sit at the table with him and Doc, but he knew it would eventually come down to them. Except for Bat Masterson, there didn't seem to be another poker player in town who could play with them at the same level.

So far he'd found his stopover in Trinidad both entertaining and dangerous. Where else would he have been able to meet Doc Holliday and the Earps? And being introduced to them by Bat Masterson had immediately put him on the inside. Wyatt had been impressive in both size and demeanor. Doc, while not physically imposing, was an imposing presence, nevertheless. As for Virgil, he'd found himself feeling sorry for him. But he didn't know if he would have been able to face the prospect of a future with one arm as courageously as Virgil was.

And, in the short time he'd been there, he felt that he and Bat had become friends—even more friendly than he'd gotten with Jim Masterson in a much longer time period in Dodge. The only man he'd come away from Dodge feeling he was friends with was Neal Brown, and he had no idea what had become of him after Dodge City.

Butler was sitting at a table playing solitaire with a fresh deck when men started entering, bellying up to the bar and surveying the place to see what was going on.

Bat made rounds of the town, settled a couple of petty disputes, and then went back to his office. The first thing he did was burn his hand when he tried to remove the deputy's badge from the stove. He didn't even know why he'd put the thing there. He had to use a kerchief to take it off, and then he laid it aside to cool off. He was lucky the damned thing hadn't melted. It would have been hell to clean, and he would have had to pay to replace it.

He made a mental note to get more deputy's stars made up.

He settled in behind his desk and wondered what kind of trouble he might get into over this phony warrant. There was certainly no one else who could have asked him for such a favor other than Wyatt Earp.

He found himself wondering exactly the same thing Butler had been wondering earlier—what was it about Wyatt Earp that commanded the friendship and loyalty of men like himself and Doc Holliday? He was not able to answer it as succinctly as Doc Holliday had.

CHAPTER 27

"That's him," Pennington said. "That's Holliday."

"Are you sure?" Seth asked.

"I seen him before," Pennington said, "around town with the Earps."

Seth looked around quickly.

"Are you sure the Earps left town?"

"Yeah," Pennington said. "I saw them."

"S-should we take him now?"

"He's right in the middle of town, Seth," Pennington said. "Walkin' down the street. How's that gonna look."

"But you said you wanted to dry gulch him."

"Yeah, but not in broad daylight when everybody can see us do it, idiot," Pennington said. "I wanna kill him, but I don't wanna go to jail for it. Understand?"

"Sure, Frank, sure," Seth said, secretly glad they weren't going to try to take Doc without Deke and Waldo. "I understand. So whatta we do?"

"You stay with him," Pennington said. "Follow him, but don't try anything until I say so. Got it?"

"I got it."

"I'm gonna find the others," Pennington said. "Just stay with him."

* * *

By the time Bat finished his rounds, went to his office, did some business at his desk, had some coffee, thought about what he was doing with the warrant and the judge, and then left his office again and walked to the Bonanza, Butler was there playing solitaire.

"Beer, Roscoe," he said to the bartender, "and one for my friend."

The head bartender put two beers on the counter and Bat took them and walked to Butler's table.

"You have a problem," he told the gambler.

"What's that, Bat?"

"You're the only person in this town I can stand to drink with."

Flattered, but not wanting to show it, Butler said, "Well, since you seem to have an extra beer with you, have a seat."

Bat sat down, put both beers on the table and slid one over to Butler's side.

"Thanks," Butler said.

They both drank down about half their beers.

"So if you don't like anybody in town, Bat, why stay?" Butler asked.

"I didn't say I don't like anyone in town," the lawman answered. "I said I can't stand to drink with 'em. And the reason I'm still in town is that I told these folks I'd be their marshal for a year. I still got more than half that time left. I always try to keep my word."

"Admirable."

"That's why I'm stuck lookin' after Doc," Bat added. "Where is Doc, by the way?"

"Hey," Butler said, "I'm not the one who said I'd keep an eye on him. Last I saw he was still walking around town. 'Taking the air,' as he said." He put a black eight on a red nine.

Bat sat back in his chair, regarding his half-full mug of beer.

"You know, there are men in this town who would back shoot him—or me—just to say they did it."

"I think Doc knows that, Bat."

"Yeah, I guess," Bat said. "I'm gonna go and check with the judge. The quicker I get that warrant the quicker Doc can be on his way."

"What about your beer?"

"Half's fine," Bat said, getting to his feet.

"Well, Doc will be here tonight to play poker." Turned over an ace, placed it on the table above the other cards.

"Good," Bat said, "at least then I'll know where he is."

"He wants to play poker, so I won't be able to man your faro table," Butler warned Bat.

"That's okay," Bat said. "I can leave it closed for another night."

"Okay." Butler placed a red queen atop a black king. "I'll see you later, then."

Bat left the saloon as others filed in. It was starting to get late and things were beginning to pick up. In another half hour there'd be girls on the floor, hawking drinks and flirting. By then somebody would be ready for a poker game.

Two hours later Butler was playing poker with three other men when Doc Holliday came through the batwing doors. Butler found himself heaving a sigh of relief. He had not seen Bat since he left to find the judge, and he was starting to worry about both of them only because of what Bat had said about back shooting, and what had happened at the Bucket of Blood. With men like Bat and Doc in town, men like Vance and his boys would always be there. Just because they'd killed six of them didn't mean there weren't any left.

Doc got a whiskey from the bartender, walked over and said, "Mind if I sit in?"

Butler had warned the players that he was keeping a seat open for Doc, and none of them seemed to mind.

"That's your chair," one of them said. "Butler's been savin' it for you. Guess you fellas had a previous engagement. Hope the rest of us ain't in the way."

"You might be," Doc said, sitting down and placing his drink carefully on the table, "but not for very long."

CHAPTER 28

━━━◆━━━

Bat Masterson came in after Doc had been playing poker for about an hour. He exchanged a nod with Butler. Doc didn't look up but Butler was sure he'd seen Bat enter. One of the girls, a very cute blonde with blue eyes and almost translucent skin, was in the act of placing another whiskey by Doc's elbow.

"Thank you, my dear," he said.

"Sure thing, Doc."

She walked away and Doc did not even look up to watch her, as the other men did. Even Butler had to sneak a look. It was this kind of concentration that made him such a good poker player.

Butler had not counted Doc's drink. He found out the day before that it didn't matter. Doc Holliday was going to be Doc Holliday no matter what anybody said. The drinking did seem to affect his ability to walk, but not his ability to play cards.

Bat went to the bar, got himself a beer, then turned, leaned against the bar, and watched the game. Other games were going on around them, but it was the table with Ty Butler and Doc Holliday—and those other

three guys—that was attracting most of the attention.
  Even from outside.

Seth Cates was watching the game through the front
window. He'd followed Doc around all day, when all
the man seemed to want to do was walk. Finally, he'd
gone back to his hotel where he had spent hours. Seth
had waited across the street, desperate for Pennington
and the others to join him. If Doc Holliday saw him he'd
be a dead man.
  Finally, Doc had come out of his hotel and walked
over to the saloon. Now, as Seth peered in the window,
it was dark, so at least he had that cover going for him.
  But where the hell were the others?

Pennington was drinking in the Bucket of Blood with
Deke and Waldo. He was on his third beer since it had
gotten dark.
  "Frank?" Deke said.
  "Huh?"
  "Shouldn't we go and find Seth now?" he asked. "Find
out where Holliday is?"
  "Yeah," Pennington said, "yeah, we should. But you
know what?"
  "What?"
  "I been thinkin'."
  "About what?" Waldo asked.
  "Maybe we shouldn't bushwack Holliday."
  "We shouldn't?" Waldo asked.
  "No."
  "Why not?" Deke asked.
  "Because we get ourselves a bigger and better rep by
killin' him face-to-face."
  "Face-to-face?" Deke asked.

"With Doc Holliday?" Waldo asked. "Are you crazy."

"No," Pennington said, "listen to me. He plays poker all night, and drinks while he does it. We get him when he's drunk, when he's about to leave the saloon."

"Outside?" Waldo asked. "In the dark?"

"No," Pennington said, "inside, so we can see."

"What about Masterson?" Deke asked. "And the gambler?"

"It'll be a fair fight," Pennington said. "They'll stay out of it."

"Fair fight?" Deke asked. "Four against one?"

"See?" Pennington said, "There's four of us, and we're all pretty good with a gun, right?"

"Well . . ." Deke said.

"Four against one," Pennington said. "We ain't gonna get better odds than that."

Deke and Waldo looked at each other, wondering if it was Pennington who was drunk.

"I'm serious," Pennington said, "and I'm sober." He pushed the remainder of his third beer away and held out his hand. "See? Steady as a rock."

Pennington could see he was still going to have to convince the two of them, so he went to the bar and got them each a beer.

"Now listen," he said, when they each had a beer in their hands . . .

One by one the other players fell by the wayside again, as they had the night before, leaving Butler and Doc the last two players in the game.

"Well," Doc said, "head-to-head again."

"Looks that way."

"Want to go ahead and play this time?"

Men all around them leaned in to hear the answer. If these two were going to play head-to-head poker, it was going to be something to watch.

"Don't know when we'll get this chance again," Doc said. "I may be leavin' town tomorrow."

"Headin' for Denver?"

"Who knows," Doc asked. "I may be headin' for boot hill."

"Well," Butler said, "if that's the case"—he paused to check his watch, then tucked it back into his vest—"it's early yet. Let's go head-to-head."

CHAPTER 29

In time, as the hands went by, a circle formed around the table. Even Bat Masterson had to move in closer to watch what was going on.

Outside the saloon Seth Cates began to get concerned when he couldn't see anything. He was trying to decide what to do—making decisions was not his strong suit—when Pennington and the others showed up.

"It's about time," he complained.

"Shut up," Pennington said, looking in the window. "What's goin' on in there?"

"Doc Holliday and that gambler, Butler, are playin' five-card stud head-to-head."

"We can't see nothin' from out here," Deke complained.

"That's why we're gonna go inside and join the party, Deke," Pennington said, slapping him on the back.

"We're goin' in?" Seth asked, puzzled.

"Waldo," Pennington said, "explain the plan to Seth, and then the two of you come in and join us."

As Pennington went into the saloon with Deke close at his heels, Seth turned to Waldo and asked, "What plan?"

* * *

Butler looked down at his cards. His hole card was a king. One of his up cards was a king. Across from him Doc Holliday was showing two aces. If he had a third in the hole—or even another pair—Butler was dead.

But they each only had four cards. There was a fifth to come.

Doc had bet three hundred, and was waiting for Butler to call or fold. Or raise.

"Make it six hundred," Butler said.

"You're bettin' like you already have a third king," Doc said.

"Aren't you betting like you already have a third ace?"

Doc was the dealer. He held the deck in his left hand, pushed his money out with his right.

"Call."

He dealt them each their fifth card.

King for Butler.

Ace for Doc.

The crowd gasped. Bat Masterson shook his head.

"Looks like this is the make or break hand, Doc," Butler said.

"Looks like it," Doc said, setting the now useless deck down.

Bat did not imagine how either one of them could get away from this hand. You just couldn't lay a hand like this down in five-card stud, and he didn't even know what their hole cards were. At that moment, though, he most certainly would rather have been in Doc's chair than in Butler's.

Butler knew there was no getting away from this hand. There was also going to be no bluffing. This was just a matter of who had the best cards, with all the money go-ing into the middle of the table because, at that moment, they were about even.

Doc also knew there was no folding now. This is the hand poker players wait for, only they both had it. The question was, who had the better dream hand?

Butler had three kings on the table with a deuce of spades keeping them company.

Doc had three aces on the table with a seven of clubs alongside them to tag along.

Everyone watching was leaning forward, waiting for the next play to be made.

"Three aces are high on the table," Doc said. "It's my bet."

"Yeah, it is," Butler said, sitting back in his chair. Despite some distractions in the room, he'd been able to concentrate for the most part. He hoped the same was true of Doc.

Everyone waited for the bet.

Pennington was waiting also. Despite himself he had managed to get caught up in the game. Deke was stand-ing next to him, also watching the two men intently.

Behind them, outside the circle of onlookers, Waldo was still trying to convince Seth that the plan was sound—this despite the fact that he still was not con-vinced himself.

Still, it was his responsibility to make sure Seth knew his part.

"That's a pretty good-looking hand you got there, Doc," Butler said.

"Yours ain't bad, either, old son."

"No, it ain't," Butler agreed. "I'd go to the mat every time with a hand like this."

"Exactly how I feel about mine."

"So what do we do?" Butler asked.

Finally, Doc Holliday pushed all his money into the center of the table and said, "I guess we go for it all."

CHAPTER 30

———◆◆◆———

Jesus, Bat thought, is Butler gonna do it—go for it all against three aces on the table? Sure, he had three kings, but that was second best against Doc's aces.

Unless Butler had another one in the hole—or a deuce.

Bat had been involved in hands like this himself, but he'd found those less nerve-wracking than this one.

If either man lost, would it break them? Financially and in spirit?

Would Doc Holliday go over the edge?

How would Butler react?

His feeling was that the hand was worse for everyone watching than for the two men involved. To them this was just one more hand, no more or less important than any that had come before, or would come later.

Anyway, that's how Bat would have approached. Many was the time he'd been beaten in a hand like this and left for broke. He always managed to come back. He always managed to find himself in a hand like this again, and come out on top next time.

Until the next time . . .

* * *

Butler looked at all the money in the middle of the table.
Losing this hand would not break him, but he wondered
if it would break Doc? It didn't really matter. He was
going to play the hand to win, no matter what. He was
just wondering . . .

"Jesus Christ!" Bat Masterson yelled. "What's it gonna
be?"

Other men began yelling, and they didn't stop until
Butler put his hands in his chips.

Then it got dead quiet.

Doc Holliday watched without emotion. He believed
that he had spit up all the emotion he had left inside of
him. There was nothing left really. Now his life was just
like this poker game, just waiting to see what the next
move was going to be.

"Okay," Butler said, shoving the remainder of his chips
into the center of the table with Doc's, "I call."

Now the onlookers leaned in to see the hole cards of
the two players.

"What do you have, Doc?" Butler asked.

"You're lookin' at them," Doc Holliday said. "Three
aces. If you got a fourth king in the hole, you got me."

"No king," Butler said, turning over his hole card,
"but would another deuce do?"

"Full house!" somebody exclaimed in a hushed tone.

Doc Holliday stared across the table at Butler and
said, "Nice hand, old son. How about a drink?"

"Okay, game's over," Bat shouted. "Give the gents
some room."

Men started to move away, back to their own tables,
or to the bar, or even out the front doors. Butler raked

his money in and two girls came over to take the chips away and cash them in.

"Let's have that drink at the bar," Doc suggested. "Bat, would you care to join us?"

"Sure," Bat said.

The three men went to the bar. Bat and Butler ordered beer, while Doc stuck with whiskey.

"To the victor," he said, raising his shot glass.

"That was some hand," Bat said.

"Yes, it was," Doc said. "I've seen our friend bluff before, but he wasn't bluffing this time."

"No, he wasn't," Bat said.

Butler didn't comment. To him there was no way to bluff that hand. Most of what they had was on the table.

Doc finished his drink and signaled the bartender for another. Bat and Butler nursed their beers.

"Whew," someone said from down the bar, "that Doc Holliday sure got skunked in that game!"

Butler cringed, Bat craned his neck to see who was speaking. Doc ignored the comment.

"I mean, it was pretty clear who had the winning hand that time," the voice said. "Didn't take a blind man to see that."

Doc accepted his fresh drink from the bartender. Butler watched him as he downed it with a steady hand.

"Doc Holliday sure must be losin' it," the man's voice said. "But then what do you expect from a lunger. He probably coughed up most of the brains he ever had."

"Okay, that's enough," Bat shouted. He turned to face that end of the bar. "Who's got the big mouth?"

The men between him and the speaker backed away from the bar. Frank Pennington stood at the end with his three partners right behind him.

"I'm just havin' my opinion, Marshal," Pennington said.

"Christ, Pennington, is that you? Man, you ain't got the brains God gave a donkey."

Pennington stiffened, and his face reddened.

"I ain't havin' words with you, Marshal," he said. "I was talkin' about Holliday."

"I know," Bat said. "That's why I know you ain't got no brains. Why would you wanna go and poke at a man who just lost a bunch of money on a tough hand—"

Bat stopped short when he felt a hand on his arm.

"It's okay, Masterson," Holliday said. "I can handle this."

"Doc, I'm the law—"

"Don't worry," Doc said, "I'm not gonna press charges. I'm just gonna have a talk with these waddies."

"I ain't no waddie!" Pennington snapped, straightening up, his hand hanging down by his gun. The three men behind him all straightened and spread their legs, but Bat, Butler, and Doc could see the fear on their faces. The question was, who did they fear more, Pennington or Doc Holliday?

CHAPTER 31

"You're obviously lookin' for a fight, friend," Doc Holliday said. "I just lost a lot of money, so lucky for you I'm in the mood for a fight."

Suddenly, the bar became the place not to be. As had happened in the Bucket of Blood some nights ago, men began to find someplace else in the room to be—or they left the saloon altogether. For the most part, however, they wanted to see this showdown, so tables were upturned and used for cover, or men just hit the floor but kept their heads up so they could see what was happening.

Bat didn't move, except to give Doc some space. Butler was behind Doc's right shoulder, at the end of the bar. He could see Doc's face in profile, and he could see his neck. He wondered if Bat was seeing what he was. There was a coughing fit in Doc that was trying to get out, but Doc was trying to hold it in until after he dealt with Pennington and his men.

"Come on, lunger," Pennington sneered, "I ain't afraid of you, neither are my boys."

"Four against one," Doc said. "That sound like good odds to you, Bat?"

"I can't let this happen, Pennington," Bat stated, but again it was Doc who called him off.

"Don't worry, Marshal," Holliday said, "they won't draw unless I turn my back."

Stung, Pennington brought his hand back, as if he was ready to draw, but it looked like more of a pose than anything else. Butler thought that Doc was going to be able to talk these boys out of drawing on him—but then it happened. The cough Doc had been trying to suppress came up, and there was nothing he could do about it. Before he knew it he was in its grip, racked by spasms of choking that seemed to disconnect his arms and legs. He staggered, caught himself on the bar. and hung there, halfway between standing and falling.

Frank Pennington saw his chance. His eyes widened, he couldn't believe his luck, and he yelled to his boys, "Take 'im now," and they were ready, too. The sight of Doc hanging off the end of the bar emboldened them, and the four men went for their guns.

But Butler, who had been expecting the fit, was moving already. He pushed off from the bar with his left hand and drew his gun with his right. His concentration was so focused on the four men, who in turn were intent on killing Doc Holliday, that none of them saw Bat Masterson also draw his weapon.

Butler and Bat both knew that Doc was a sitting duck, and they had to move both swiftly and with deadly accuracy.

Butler shot Pennington first, taking him square in the chest, and then moved his gun a fraction to fire at one of the other men.

Bat fired twice in succession, and two men gasped and staggered back. They righted themselves briefly, but then Butler's lead hit them and put them down.

The fourth man was stunned by what was happening and was riddled by lead from both Bat's gun and Butler's.

As the four men hit the floor Butler quickly stepped in front of Doc, in case one of them was able to fire a shot from there. Bat, meanwhile, moved in on them, gun ready. If any of them was still alive they would not be for long. If Bat hated anything it was a bushwacker, and shooting Doc while he was in the throes of a coughing fit amounted to the same thing.

"Doc," Butler said, reaching back with one hand to steady the man. "You okay?"

"I'm not hit if that's what you mean," Doc said in a raspy tone. "Damn." He looked at the bartender. "Whiskey!"

"Comin' up, Doc," Roscoe said, and got a shot glass of rotgut in front of him fast.

Doc grabbed it, downed it, and released the edge of the bar. He staggered, but remained standing.

Bat came over and said, "They're all dead."

"I'm obliged to the both of you," Doc said. "I would have handled them if not for . . . this." He patted his chest.

"We know that, Doc," Butler said. He and Bat replaced the spent shells in their guns and holstered them.

"Roscoe," Bat said. "Grab some men and get these bodies out of here."

"The undertaker?" Roscoe asked.

"Yeah," Bat said. "There's only four of 'em. He should have room."

"He might be asleep."

"Wake him up, then."

"Yes, sir."

Bat turned to Doc.

"You're not hit?"

"Not hit," Doc said. "Just a little . . . chagrined, I guess you'd say. Not used to havin' somebody else fight my battles for me. You two acted pretty damn quick."

"It's my job," Bat said.

"I saw you were having trouble breathing," Butler said, "knew that a cough was coming."

"You're very observant," Doc said. "I thank you both again. I think I better go back to my hotel now."

"Sure, Doc," Butler said. "Want me to—"

"I think I can manage on my own, tonight."

Butler nodded and stepped back.

Doc looked at Bat.

"Any word on that warrant?"

"I'm gonna pick it up in the mornin'," Bat said. "I can bring it to your hotel."

"Any objection to me leavin' tomorrow, then?" Doc asked.

"None."

Doc smiled without humor.

"Probably glad to see the back of me."

"As a lawman," Bat said, "I'd have to agree with that."

"I understand. Good night to both of you. See you tomorrow before I head out."

"'Night, Doc," Butler said.

Doc Holliday went out the door, following the men who were carrying the bodies.

"You really saw that he was gonna cough?" Bat asked.

"Yeah," Butler said. "You didn't?"

"I couldn't see his face," Bat said. "I just knew when he started to cough those jackals would try to take advantage. You move pretty fast for a gambler."

"You move as fast as your rep says you do," Butler said.

Bat looked around the room. Men were righting tables, setting up chairs, calling for drinks from the girls, whose eyes were still wide from what had happened.

Roscoe, having arranged to have the bodies removed, stepped back behind the bar and began taking orders.

"Looks like things are getting back to normal," Bat said.

"I think I've had enough for one night," Butler said. "I'm gonna go to my room."

"Don't blame you," Bat said. "I'm gonna stick around for a while. You gonna see Holliday off in the morning?"

"I think so," Butler said. "I kinda feel like we became friends, you know?"

"Sure, I know," Bat said. "I don't feel the same way, but I understand why you do. Good night, Butler."

"'Night, Bat."

"Thanks for back up . . . again."

Butler grinned and said, "Any time."

CHAPTER 32

One Month Later,
Denver

When Butler hit Denver he heaved a sigh. He didn't know if it was of relief exactly, but it was nice to be in a city for a change after all the mining camps and towns.

He'd stayed in Trinidad longer than he'd expected, but now it was time to stay in Denver for a while. His luck was still running good, and there was the possibility of getting into some big games here.

As he checked into the Denver House Hotel he knew that the Earps had moved on to Gunnison, Colorado. Wyatt had sent Bat a telegram to that effect after Bat notified him that the Doc Holliday favor had been done.

As for Doc Holliday they had not heard from him since he'd left Trinidad, ostensibly for Denver. Who knew what stops he might have made along the way?

Butler had personal knowledge of all the stops that could have been made, but he made none of them. He was that intent on making it to Denver.

Now he took his key and made his way to his second-floor room. He paused halfway up the steps to turn and look down at the wide expanse of lobby below him. This was certainly not Trinidad—or Leadville.

He was very happy with his room. It was large, well furnished, and the mattress was plush and comfortable. He walked to the window and looked out at the busy street below him. He hadn't been any place this populated since Chicago, and that was a while ago.

He decided to have a long bath, put on some new clothes, and go out to greet the city—or let it greet him.

Perry Mallon stopped just inside the door of the saloon and scanned the room quickly. He found what he was looking for without a problem. A member of the Denver Police Department, Mallon was in uniform, wearing a gun, and carrying a billy club. He turned, looked outside, and jerked his head at the others to follow him in. In seconds he was one of four policemen standing inside the door. The place was fairly quiet, just a murmur of voices and the sound of poker chips. Slowly, the four policemen attracted the attention of some of the patrons— most of them curious, some of them nervous. What had brought four lawmen into the Gambler's Club?

Len Wooden, the owner, approached the four uniformed men and said, "What can I do for you officers?"

Mallon put the head of his club against Wooden's chest.

"Just stay out of the way, friend," he said. "We're here to see one of your patrons."

Wooden frowned. He longed for the days of a sheriff and a deputy. These bully boys in uniforms didn't take long to develop an attitude. This one looked new, and he had it already.

Wooden looked around the room, and his eyes fell on one man. Suddenly, he understood. "Can we do this without fuss?" he asked the policeman.

"Just go and get behind your bar," Mallon said. "We'll take care of it any way we have to."

"Jesus," Wooden said, and withdrew. He could have warned some of his better customers, but instead headed straight for the safety of the bar. At the first sign of trouble he could simply drop out of sight, out of harm's way.

Mallon waved his three colleagues to follow him and headed for the table across the room. The man he was interested in was sitting with his back to the wall, and for all intents and purposes had not seen the four policemen. But as soon as they reached the table, he looked up and locked eyes with Perry Mallon.

"Up," Mallon said.

"Excuse me?"

"You heard me," Mallon said. "Stand up." He was bouncing the billy club off the palm of his hand.

"What's this about?"

"I think you know."

The seated man frowned.

"Do I know you?"

"Think about it."

The gambler sat back, looked up at Mallon, and frowned.

"I don't think I know you."

"Well, you'll have time to think about it in a cell," Mallon said. "Come on. Let's go."

"What's the charge?"

"We'll let you know."

The gambler looked down at his cards and chips.

"I'll have to cash out."

"Somebody will do that for you," Mallon said.

The other three policemen were watching the byplay tensely. Mallon had told them he could handle it, and just wanted them there for backup. All three were hefting their clubs, and hoping they wouldn't have to use their guns.

"Don't make this hard," Mallon said. "It won't go your way."

"Oh," the black-clad gambler said, "it might."

One of the other men leaned forward and said, "I'll cash in your chips and hold the money for ya, Doc."

Doc Holliday looked at the man. His name was Benny Keats, and Doc was only in the game because of him. Could he trust him with his money? He probably could, since the little man was afraid of him.

"Okay, Benny," Doc said. "You do that. And remember, I know exactly how much I have."

"S-sure."

"That's enough talk, Doc," Police Officer Perry Mallon said. "Get up. You're under arrest."

CHAPTER 33

————◆————

Butler dressed for dinner, something else he hadn't done since Chicago. He asked the desk clerk to recommend a place for a good steak and the man sent him three blocks away to a place called Seldon's Steak House. It was very crowded, but since he was dining alone he was able to be seated almost immediately. Around him were mostly tables of two, three, and four. A lot of them were families, some of them couples. Other tables were obviously friends out for dinner together.

Butler ordered a steak with the works, and while he was waiting for it he saw a woman enter. She spoke briefly to the host, who was shaking his head. Butler assumed that he was turning the woman away, and she looked dismayed. Beautiful, and dismayed. He decided to be chivalrous tonight.

He stood up and walked across the room. As he got closer the woman got even lovelier. Also, older. At first he thought she was in her late twenties, but now it appeared she was in her thirties.

". . . sorry, Madam," the host was saying, "but I simply cannot seat a woman alone."

"But that's archaic," she insisted. "My money is as good as anyone else's, and I'm hungry."

She had obviously also dressed for dinner. She wore a green wrap over a dress of the same color, which set off her red hair and pale skin. Her eyes were green, and they were flashing.

"I sent a bellboy over this afternoon to make a reservation," she said. "J. Conway."

"Yes," the man said, "we have a reservation for a J. Conway, but we did not know it was a woman."

"Jennifer Conway," she said. "What's the damn difference?" She almost stamped her foot.

"Madam," he said, "if you're going to use profanity I'm going to have to ask you to—"

"Jennifer, there you are," Butler said.

Both she and the host looked at him with frowns. He came up next to her, touched her arm, and pecked her cheek.

"I told you that you wouldn't be able to get in on your own," he said. "Now come and sit with me like we planned."

"I—but—but—" she said.

He leaned in and said, "You can stand up for yourself and starve or sit with me and eat."

"Darling," she said, "you were right, after all. There are some aspects of Denver that are still backwater."

Butler laughed to himself. She had to get a parting shot in.

"If you don't mind," he said to the host, "I'll take Miss Conway to my table now."

"Of course, sir," the host said stiffly.

Butler kept a hold of the woman's arm as they walked across the floor.

"Did you come here for a steak?" he asked.

"Yes," she said, "the desk clerk at my hotel told me they serve the best steaks in town."

Butler caught his waiter even before they reached their table and said, "Bring two steak dinners, please."

"Yes, sir."

When they reached the table Butler held her chair for her, inhaling the scent of her perfume at the same time.

"Since we seem to be a couple," she said, "and you somehow know my name—"

"I overheard you tell the host."

"—I suppose you ought to tell me your name."

"I'm sorry," he said. "Bad manners. I'm Tyrone Butler."

"I'm going to assume, Mr. Butler, since you are dining alone that you're not from Denver?"

"That's correct," he said, "and please don't call me Mister. Either Ty or just Butler will do."

"Well then, for the sake of appearances, you might as well call me Jennifer."

"So, Jennifer," he said, "two strangers dining together. What shall we talk about?"

"Well, Ty," she replied, "as you say we're strangers, so I suppose we should talk about . . . everything."

CHAPTER 34

They did talk about everything—and found out just how much they had in common. Both had come from the East—she more recently than he. They had each lost contact with all family members, although neither said how or why. They both wanted to see as much of the West as they possibly could. Both had just arrived that day, and both were staying at the Denver House.

He also discovered that she was a very progressive woman. She thought women should have all the same rights as men—from eating alone in restaurants to voting.

Butler didn't see why a woman shouldn't eat alone in a restaurant if she wanted to, but voting was another matter and he didn't comment on that.

They agreed that the steaks were among the finest they'd ever had. He said he'd had a better one in Chicago, and she said she'd had one in Boston that was more succulent.

After dinner they each ordered coffee and dessert, cherry pie for him and apple for her.

"So tell me, Ty," she said, "how long do you intend to stay in Denver?"

"I don't know," he said. "I don't usually plan that far in advance. I guess I'll stay until I've seen what I can see and am ready to move on."

"Hmm, I'm afraid my plans are a little more rigid than that. I have three days here and then I move on to Salt Lake City."

"Do you have friends there?"

"No," she said, "and no family. I don't know a soul there. I just want to see it."

"And eat alone."

"Yes." She smiled. "I have had trouble with that everywhere I've gone, but I have to thank you again for getting me in here. I may not have eaten alone, but I've enjoyed the meal and the company."

"Same here."

When they were finished with the entire dinner, Butler insisted on paying. She argued until he reminded her that they had to keep up appearances.

Since they were staying in the same hotel, it was only natural to walk back together.

"You haven't told me what you do for a living," she said.

"I don't think you asked until now," he said. "I play poker."

"You gamble for a living?"

"I play poker for a living," he said. "I'm very good at it, so I don't really consider it gambling."

"Really? You win all the time?"

"I don't win all the time," he said. "Nobody does. But I win more than I lose, and I manage to make a living."

"That's fascinating."

"Now you haven't told me what you do."

"I'm a writer."

"Really? What do you write?"

"Articles, mostly," she said. "I send them to magazines and newspapers."

"And you make a living that way?" he asked. "Now, I find that pretty fascinating."

"Well, I have to admit," she said, "I have only had a few pieces published. I'm actually traveling on money that I've saved over the years. I'm not a young girl, and I have worked many jobs over the years to save money. And . . ." She hesitated, then let it out. "I have a small inheritance."

"Well," he said, "that's always helpful."

"I hesitated to say that," she said. "I'm not rich by any means, but I am able to travel as I want."

"I think that's fine."

"I just didn't want you to think I was this rich, pampered woman," she explained. "I really do want to write for a living, but I can't get many publications to print my articles."

"Because of your progressive views?"

"Exactly."

"Have you thought of writing other things?"

"Like what?"

"I don't know . . . travelogues describing places you've been, things you've done?"

"I suppose I could do that," she said, "and still get my views across. I have to be true to my beliefs, you know."

"Of course," he said. "We all have to do that."

It was dark, but the streets of Denver were well lit by street lamps. She peered at him anxiously.

"You're not making fun of me, are you?"

"I wouldn't do that," he said. "I have no reason to do that. I think everything you've said is admirable."

"Then you're a special man," she said. "Most men I've

spoken to think I'm crazy, or stupid. They think I should be married and in some man's kitchen—or bed."

Her face grew red when she said that, and she put her hand over her mouth.

"I'm sorry," she said. "That just popped out."

"It's okay," he told her. "I don't shock easily."

When they reached the hotel and entered the bright lobby, he asked her, "Would you like a nightcap in the bar?"

"I don't think so," she said. "I've taken up enough of your time, and I don't want to scandalize whoever may be in there. Besides, I'd like to do some writing tonight before I go to sleep. Again, thank you so much for a lovely evening."

"The pleasure was all mine." He took her hand and kissed it.

"You're very gallant," she said. "I hope we'll see each other again."

"I was actually planning on it," he told her.

He watched as she walked up the steps to the second floor, then turned and went into the bar.

CHAPTER 35

————◆◉◆————

Butler entered the hotel bar and stopped a moment, to be impressed by the crystal, mahogany, and the green felt. He walked up to the bar, where a bartender wearing a vest and a bow tie greeted him.

"Welcome, sir. Guest in the hotel?"

"That's right."

"What'll you have?"

"A beer."

"Comin' up."

He turned while waiting to examine the clientele. From his vantage point he could not see a gun. His own was in a holster beneath his left arm. Most of them were wearing suits like his own, some brown, some blue, others black. They were speaking in low tones. There were no girls working the floor, and there was no music, and no gambling.

A quiet saloon, he thought. What a concept.

"Here you go, sir," the bartender said.

Perfect color, perfect head, and ice cold. He had died and gone to heaven. If he needed any more proof of that, he needed only to look to his dinner companion, who he hoped to see more of in the next few days.

He sipped his beer and keyed in on a conversation that was taking place between two men at the table nearest to him.

". . . walked right in, interrupted his poker game, and arrested him," one man was saying.

"Are you sure it was him?" the other man asked.

"Hell, that's what I heard."

"How do we find out for sure?"

They both craned their necks and looked around.

"How about we ask the bartender," the second man asked. "Those guys know everything."

"Yeah, let's do that."

Both men stood up and approached the bar, which put them right next to Butler.

"Hey, barkeep," the first man called.

Both men looked like businessmen with money, having a drink after work. Butler would have bet they were regulars here.

"What can I get for you gents?" the bartender asked.

"We got a question for you," the man said. "We heard that Doc Holliday is in Denver, and that he was arrested earlier today."

Butler's ears perked up. He put his beer on the bar and forgot about it.

"That's what I heard, gents."

"We also heard they took him right out of a poker game."

"Yup."

"See?" the first man said to his companion. "I told you."

They went back to their table, satisfied with the answer.

"Bartender?" Butler said.

"Sir?"

"Do you have any more information on Doc Holliday's arrest?"

"Just what I heard, sir," the bartender said. "He was playing poker, the police came in and arrested him. Took him right out of the game."

"He went peacefully?"

"That's what I heard," the man said. "What's your interest?"

"I know him."

"Doc Holliday?" The bartender looked impressed. "You know Doc Holliday?"

"Shhh," Butler said. "Keep your voice down. Yes, we're . . . friends, sort of."

"Jeez," the young man said, "friends with Doc Holliday. Did you come here to meet him?"

"No," Butler said. "The fact that we're both in Denver is a coincidence."

"Well . . . I'm sorry you had to hear about it like this."

"Where would they have taken him?"

"Police headquarters, I guess, over on Cherokee Street—but you'll never get in there at this time of night."

"You're probably right."

"If you want to see him you're better off waiting until tomorrow morning." The man grabbed Butler's beer. "I'll get you a fresh one, nice and cold."

"Thanks."

Butler's mind was still racing when the bartender came back and put the fresh beer in front of him.

"What's your name, friend?" Butler asked.

"Jeremy."

"Here's to you, Jeremy," Butler said, and took a healthy swallow.

"So where do you know Doc Holliday from?" Jeremy asked.

"Trinidad."

"I know where that is. South, right?"

"Right."

"Have you been to Tombstone?"

"No," Butler said. "I wasn't there." And he didn't add that he also knew the Mastersons and the Earps. Better to keep all that quiet.

"I just happened to be in Trinidad when Doc came to town, and we played some poker." Butler looked into his beer, seemed to find another question there. "Say, you didn't happen to hear what Doc was arrested for, did you?"

"Well . . ."

"Come on, Jeremy," Butler said. "Don't hold out on me now."

"I heard it was murder," Jeremy said. "Something about sending him back to Arizona."

There it was. Now Butler knew there was one thing he was going to have to do even before he went to see Doc.

Send Bat Masterson a telegram.

CHAPTER 36

Doc Holliday looked up at Perry Mallon, who was standing over him with his billy club. It was early and Doc had been in jail all night. His suit was rumpled, his face covered by stubble, and his breathing was ragged. He'd had several coughing fits during the night that had left him weak and, if it hadn't been for a concerned guard who had brought him water a time or two, he might have choked to death. But now he simply sat in his seat and stared at Mallon with bloodshot eyes, his hands handcuffed in front of him.

"Keep lookin' at me like that, Holliday," Mallon said. "See how much good it does you?"

"What've you got against me, Mallon?" Holliday asked. "Is it because we've met but I don't remember you? I meet a lot of people, you know. I can't remember every one I meet, or every cockroach I step on."

Mallon pulled the billy club back, preparing to use it on Doc, when the metal door to the room opened and an older man stepped in. Mallon quickly dropped the club.

"Mallon," the man said, "this is the man?"

"Yes, sir."

The older man stared at Doc.

"The famous killer, Doc Holliday?"

Doc didn't answer, so Mallon said, "It's him, sir. I know him."

The man looked at Mallon.

"That's right," he said. "You were there, right?"

"Yes, sir, I was there."

"In Tombstone."

"Yes, sir."

"Who are you?" Doc asked.

The older man looked at him.

"Are you talking to me?"

"Yes, I am," Doc Holliday said. "I want to know who you are."

"I am the chief of this police department," the man said, "and I don't relish having killers in my city."

"This man is a liar," Doc Holliday said.

"Is that a fact?"

"He never was in Tombstone."

"But you were," the chief said. "You are Doc Holliday, right?"

"That's right, I am."

"Then you're a killer," the chief said, "and you're going to go back and pay for your crime."

"On this man's say-so?"

"This man is one of my policemen, and he has identified you as a wanted criminal. I will contact the authorities in Arizona and you will be shipped back to stand trial."

Doc Holliday looked at the man, then looked at Perry Mallon. He knew there was no point in arguing with either one of them.

"Take him back to his cell," the chief said, "and make sure nothing happens to this man. Do you understand?"

"I understand," Mallon said.

"He's going back to Arizona in one piece."

"Yes, sir."

The man turned and left the room.

"Guess he ruined all your fun, huh, Mallon?"

"Shut up, Doc," Mallon said. "You can still accidentally fall down a flight of stairs, you know."

"Might be better than goin' back to Tombstone to hang," Doc said.

"Don't worry, Holliday," Mallon said, pulling Doc to his feet and shoving him toward the door, "you're goin' back."

Butler left the hotel and, following the directions of the desk clerk, made his way to the nearest telegraph office. He wrote out a short note to Bat Masterson, and then had the key operator send it to Trinidad.

"Will you wait for an answer, sir?" the man asked.

"I'm at the Denver House Hotel," Butler said. "Send the reply there. If I'm not around they'll hold it for me."

"Yes, sir."

Butler left the telegraph office, waved down a passing cab, and gave the driver his destination.

Police Headquarters.

He walked in and announced to the policeman at the front desk that he wanted to see Doc Holliday.

"Are you related, sir?" the man asked.

"No."

"Are you his lawyer?"

"No."

"Are you a law officer?"

"No, I'm . . . a friend of his."

"Let me check. Please have a seat."

Butler sat on a bench in the lobby . . . and sat . . . and sat . . . and finally a man came out to see him. Portly, white-haired, and obviously important.

"My name is Arthur Coolidge. I'm the chief of police here. I understand you want to see Doc Holliday?"

"That's right," Butler said. "My name is—"

"I don't care what your name is," Coolidge said. "You're obviously of the same ilk as Holliday, so I want you and your friends to know something. I'm sending him back to Arizona to answer for his crimes. Anyone who tries to stop this will also end up in my jail. Have you got that?"

"Yes, but—"

"That's all I have to say to you, sir," Coolidge said. "Good day—and get out of my police station."

It was obvious that Butler was not going to be able to see Doc Holliday, or help him, so he was going to have to try and find that help somewhere else.

He turned and left.

CHAPTER 37

When Butler got back to his hotel, there was a telegram waiting for him from Bat Masterson. It said: **AM ON THE FIRST TRAIN.**

So there was nothing he could do until Bat arrived. As a Colorado lawman armed with a warrant he might be able to keep Doc from being extradited back to Arizona. If not, then there might be something they could do together to keep it from happening.

Butler wondered where the Earps were. Last he heard they had gone to Gunnison, but whether or not they were still there he didn't know. Still, if he sent another telegram and they were there, he knew they'd head for Denver right away. He decided there could be no harm in sending it.

"Ty!"

He turned and saw Jennifer Conway coming across the lobby toward him, looking as lovely as ever, if somewhat less dressed up.

"I'm so glad I caught you," she said. "I was about to go for a walk. Would you like to join me?"

"I would like nothing better, Jennifer," he said, "but I can't. I . . . have to send a telegram."

"Oh." She was obviously disappointed, and he knew it sounded like a lame excuse.

"No, really, something came up. Uh, last night a friend of mine was arrested."

"Oh, I'm sorry. Oh, wait. I think I read something in the newspaper. Was that . . . Doc Holliday?"

"Yes, it was," he said. He hadn't seen the newspaper yet. "It's already in the paper?"

"Oh, yes, it made quite a splash. Are you hoping to help him . . . escape?" she asked.

"Nothing so dramatic," he said. "I am hoping to keep him from being sent back to Arizona, though."

"And you can do that by sending telegrams?"

"Possibly."

"Well . . . don't you have to walk to the telegraph office?"

"As a matter of fact, I do."

"Can I walk with you?" she asked. "And maybe when you've finished sending your telegrams, we can take a stroll."

"That sounds like an excellent idea," he said. "As long as you don't mind waiting at the telegraph office."

"Not at all," she said, sliding her arm through his. "Actually, it's quite exciting. It'll make me feel like I'm helping, too. Shall we go?"

They walked to the telegraph office arm in arm. Jennifer offered to wait for him outside but he wouldn't hear of it. He told her to come inside with him, where he could keep an eye on her.

He wrote out his telegram while she looked over his shoulder.

"Oh my God," she murmured, "Wyatt Earp?"

"He's Doc Holliday's good friend," Butler explained.

"I know," she said. "I mean, I read about the O.K. Corral and all."

"Well, he'd want to know that Doc is in trouble."

"And he would drop everything and come?"

"In a minute."

"And who else?"

"I've already sent one to Bat Masterson," Butler said. "The last time I saw him he was a marshal in Trinidad, Colorado. I'm hoping he still is."

"And he'll come? He's friends with Doc Holliday?"

"It's kind of complicated," Butler said, finishing up his telegram. "Bat is friends with Wyatt, Doc is friends with Wyatt, they get along for the sake of Wyatt."

"Wyatt Earp must be a special man to command such loyalty from these kind of men."

Butler took the handwritten telegram to the key operator, who then sent it on to Gunnison.

"Will you wait for an answer, or shall I send it to the hotel again?" the man asked.

"The hotel, thanks," Butler said.

He stepped outside with Jennifer and took a deep breath.

"Well, there's not much else I can do for now," he said.

"How long will it take Bat Masterson to get here?"

"He's taking the train, but it will still be a few days."

"What if they decide to send Mr. Holliday back between now and then?" she asked.

"I'm gambling that it will take longer than that," Butler said. "They have to get a judge to hear his case, or at least review it, before they decide to send him back."

"So, then, I have you for the afternoon?"

He took her arm and wrapped it around him.

"Miss Conway, you have me for the entire day, if you so wish."

* * *

In his cell Doc Holliday thought over his fate. Back in Tombstone he was as good as dead, but how could he avoid being sent back there? They hadn't even brought him a lawyer yet, and even if they did, would the man bother looking for Bat Masterson or the Earps for him? Even the gambler, Butler, would help if he knew—but Doc didn't know where he was, either.

He didn't know for sure where any of his "friends" were.

CHAPTER 38

————◈————

Butler and Jennifer spent a pleasant afternoon together, strolling around Denver, taking in the sights, learning a little more about each other, and sharing a very good lunch. Every so often Butler would think about Doc sitting in a cell, maybe coughing his lungs out, and feel bad, but there was really nothing he could do . . . unless . . .

"Do you mind if I take you back to the hotel now, Jennifer?" he asked after lunch.

"Why?" she asked. "I thought we were having a good time."

"We are," he said, "but . . ."

"Are you thinking about your friend, Doc?"

"Yes," he said. "I was wondering if he had a lawyer. Then I thought, if I get him a lawyer maybe I can get in to see him that way."

"That makes sense," she said. "Let's go find your friend a lawyer."

"You want to do that?"

"It's better than sitting back at the hotel all alone."

"I thought you had some writing to do?"

"Well," she said, "I also have some living to do, though."

"That's true."

"So," she asked, holding his arm tightly, "how do we find a lawyer?"

Butler was about to say he had no idea, when something suddenly occurred to him.

"Come on," he said, "we have to go back to the hotel."

"But," she protested as he dragged her along, "I thought we were going to look for a lawyer . . ."

It was late afternoon. Butler was hoping that the local businessmen stopped by the hotel bar then as well as after work. He was also hoping that Jeremy was working behind the bar.

By the time they reached the hotel he had explained his idea to Jennifer.

"You think that some of the men who drink in the hotel bar are lawyers?" she asked.

"I think there's bound to be a lawyer in the batch," he said. "And if not, maybe somebody will know one, like the bartender."

They entered the bar, found a smattering of men sitting at tables by twos and threes.

"See?" he said. "These men have jobs they want to get away from."

"I have to admit," she said, "some of these men look like they could be lawyers. Well, except him."

There was one man sitting alone. He was short, fat, and sweaty in a rumpled suit, and was hanging over a mug of beer as if all the cares of the world were heaped on his shoulders.

When they went to the bar, Jeremy met them there with a smile.

"Who's the pretty lady, Mr. Butler?"

"Another hotel guest, Jeremy," Butler said. "Meet Jennifer."

"Ma'am," Jeremy said. "What can I get for you?"

"How about a glass of brandy?"

"Comin' up," Jeremy said. "Beer, Butler?"

"Thanks."

When Jeremy returned with their drinks, Butler said, "I've got a problem, Jeremy."

"What's that?"

"I need a lawyer."

"Did you get into trouble already?"

"It's not for me," Butler said.

"Oh, you mean for Doc Holliday?"

"That's right," Butler said. "Do you know if any of these fellas in here is a lawyer?"

"There's a few of them in here," Jeremy said, "but there's only one you really want."

"Why is that?" Jennifer asked.

"He's the only one who takes criminal cases," Jeremy said. "Most of the offices around here are for bank or real estate lawyers."

"So there's one criminal lawyer in here?" Butler asked.

"Yes."

"Is he any good?"

"He used to be very good," Jeremy said, "but I have admit he's slipped some over the years. Now he spends a lot of his time in here."

Butler turned and looked around, saw the two men who had been discussing Doc's arrest the night before.

"One of those two?"

"Them? No, they're not lawyers of any kind. They employ lawyers. No, I'm talkin' about him."

They both looked over to where he was pointing. All they saw was the fat man in the rumpled suit, his nose now almost in his beer.

"You can't mean him," Jennifer said.

"I mean him," Jeremy said. "A few years ago he was one of the best lawyers in Denver."

"And then what happened?" Butler asked.

"Same old story," the bartender said. "I've heard it a hundred times."

"Women," Butler said.

"Was it gambling?" Jennifer asked.

"Or drinking?"

"Nope," Jeremy said, "he lost a case."

"A case?" Jennifer asked.

"One case?" Butler asked.

"That's a lot," Jeremy said, "when you've never lost one."

"Wait a minute," Jennifer said, getting interested. "You mean to say he never lost a case, and when he did he became . . . that?"

"Not exactly," Jeremy said, leaning on the bar. "He lost one, then he lost another, and then a third. His confidence was shaken. He just lost his edge. Now he just comes here a few times a week."

"And the other days he's in court?" Jennifer asked.

"No," Jeremy said, "the other days he goes and sits someplace else."

"So he goes to different bars and saloons around the city and just gets drunk?" Butler asked. "And you're recommending him?"

"Oh, no," Jeremy said. "He's not drunk. He'll sit drooped over that beer all day, and then go home."

"He doesn't drink?"

"I'm not sayin' he don't drink at all," the bartender said. "I'm just sayin' he doesn't get drunk."

"So if we walk over there right now and talk to him," Jennifer asked, "he's cold sober?"

"As a judge," Jeremy said, then added, "well, not all judges." He pointed to a well-dressed man standing at the end of the bar who was obviously very drunk, almost to the point of falling over.

"He's a judge?" Jennifer asked.

"Yup."

"Okay," Butler said, "we're getting off the subject here. "What makes you think this fella over here—"

"Oliver James."

"—this Oliver James, could handle this case."

"I think he needs a case like this to get him back," Jeremy said. "A big-name client like Doc Holliday? Do him a world of good."

Butler knew he had Bat Masterson coming to town to try to get Doc out of jail. All he really needed from a lawyer was to get him in to see Doc, and to delay things long enough for Bat to get there. He didn't need a big-name, high-price lawyer for that.

"What are you thinking?" Jennifer asked.

He explained his thought process to her while Jeremy stood there and listened.

Jennifer looked at the bartender.

"Does that sound like something he could handle?"

"In the old days, he wouldn't even touch a case like that," Jeremy said. "Right now, it's probably perfect."

Jennifer and Butler exchanged a look.

"Hey," Jeremy said, with a shrug, "how much time you got to keep shopping around?"

"He's right," Butler said to Jennifer. "I don't have time to waste."

They both looked over at the man, who certainly had all the characteristics of a classic drunk.

"Okay," Butler said, "let's do it."

CHAPTER 39

Butler and Jennifer approached the man's table. It was only then that he noticed the man's eyes were open, even though his head was hanging down.

"Mr. James?"

The man's head came up and he looked directly at Butler. His eyes were clear and bright, if a bit sad.

"My name is Butler, and this is Jennifer Conway," Butler said. "We'd like to talk to you about something."

"Talk to me?" James asked. "Why?"

"Well, the bartender over there—Jeremy—tells me that you're a lawyer. I happen to be looking for a lawyer."

"Really? Well, you can't swing a dead cat around here without hitting a lawyer. Take your pick."

"It's a criminal matter, and Jeremy says that's your specialty. May we sit down and talk?"

"You can sit down," James said, "and you can talk. I can't guarantee anything will come of it."

"Fair enough."

Butler held a chair for Jennifer, then seated himself.

"A friend of mine is in jail," Butler said.

"And you need to get him out?"

"Well, I think I have that covered, but I do need to slow down the legal process until another friend of mine gets here."

"A friend in jail and a friend coming," Oliver James said. "I think I'm going to need some names before we go any further, Mr. Butler."

When his head was hanging down it was easy to misread Oliver James's age, because his hair was thinning on top. This close, however, he seemed to be nearer to forty than fifty.

"Well, the man who's in jail is Doc Holliday," Butler said, "and the man whose arrival I'm awaiting is Bat Masterson."

James stared at Butler, then looked at Jennifer.

"He's joking, right?"

"I'm afraid not, Mr. James," she said.

The lawyer looked back at Butler.

"Doc Holliday, Bat Masterson?" he repeated. "Why not bring Wyatt Earp into the mix?"

"I've already sent a telegram in an attempt to do that very thing," Butler assured him.

"And your name again?"

"Butler, Tyrone Butler."

"You're the only one I've never heard of."

"That's not a surprise."

James sat back in his chair. Pale to this point, there suddenly seemed to be red spots on his cheeks. His eyes, sad till now, seemed interested.

"And these other fellas, they're all friends of yours?"

"That's right."

"And you can count on them?"

"As long as my telegrams reach them, yes," Butler said. "Masterson is already on his way, should be here in a couple of days."

"And you need to throw some legal road blocks up until then."

"That's right."

Oliver James did some thinking, then said, "You want to do me a favor and get us some coffee? We've got to talk some more."

"I'll get it," Jennifer said, and headed for the bar.

"She'd make a good secretary," James said. "Pretty, too."

"I think she's got other plans for a career," Butler said, "but I can't argue with the second part."

"I saw something in the papers about Doc Holliday's arrest, but didn't read it," the lawyer said. "You're going to have to fill me in on why he's in jail, and why you think you can get him out . . . legally? We are talking legally, aren't we? I mean, it's not like you and Bat Masterson and Wyatt Earp are going to break him out, right?"

"There's no question of breaking him out," Butler said. "Not when there are legal avenues."

"You sound like an educated man, sir," James said.

"I was educated in the East, have been traveling west for some time," Butler explained.

"And how is it you made the acquaintance of such august company?" James asked.

"I play poker."

"Ah," James said, "a sporting man. That explains it, then. The reputations of your friends precede them."

Jennifer returned, expertly juggling three mugs of hot coffee. Butler suspected there might have been some waitressing in her past.

"Thank you, young lady," James said.

"You're welcome, Mr. James."

"I think you both better start calling me Oliver," the man said.

"You may call me Jennifer."

"Butler will do."

"All right, friend Butler," James said, "suppose you start filling in some blanks for me."

"You'll take the case?" Butler asked.

"I didn't say that," James said, "but you fill in the blanks for me and I'll let you know."

"Fair enough," Butler said. "The way I hear it Doc was playing cards last night when . . ."

CHAPTER 40

Oliver James, attorney-at-law, listened intently as Butler told his story. He sipped his coffee, never interrupted, and Butler had the feeling that the man would never forget one word. At one point when his coffee cup was empty, Jennifer got up wordlessly and got him another.

Now he sat back as Butler finished and rubbed his jaw.

"If your friend Masterson does have an outstanding warrant then there wouldn't seem to be a problem."

"I was hoping that would be the case," Butler said.

"And if he's still wearing a marshal's badge, that would also be helpful," James pointed out.

"I guess we'll have to wait to see if that's the case," Butler said. "At least he was while still in Trinidad. I don't think he'd be there if he wasn't marshal anymore."

"However," James said, "failing to extradite him, the local authorities may decided to try him here."

"For what?"

"That's a good question. Didn't your friend Masterson come up with a warrant at virtually a moment's notice?"

"I see what you mean."

"Well," James said, "the first thing I have to do is go to the jail and see my client."

"So you're taking the case?" Jennifer asked.

"Yes, young lady," James said, "I'm taking the case—for my usual fee, mind you."

"Which is?" Butler asked.

James told him.

"That shouldn't be a problem."

"Excellent!"

"But there is one more thing," Butler said.

"And what's that?"

"I have to go with you to see Doc."

"Why?"

"He's unpredictable," Butler explained. "I don't know that he'll see you without me. Also, I want to tell him that the wheels are in motion to get him out. I don't know what he'll do inside if he doesn't know that."

"Yes, yes, all right," James said. "All good points. All right, then." The fat man got to his feet. "Meet me in front of the jail in the morning."

"Tomorrow morning? Don't you have to make some arrangements first?" Butler asked.

"All I have to do is appear at the jail and tell them that I am his lawyer," James said, "and that you work for me. They'll let us in to see your friend, and then we can truly get the wheels turning."

CHAPTER 41

Butler had to be impressed with Oliver James's demeanor at the police station the next morning. He did as he said he was going to do. He presented himself as Doc Holliday's lawyer, Butler as a man who worked for him, and now they were on their way to Doc's cell to talk to him.

When they reached the cell Doc was sitting on a cot, staring off into space. In his right hand was a well-used, bloodstained kerchief. He looked up when the uniformed policeman put his key into the lock.

"And who might you—Butler?" Doc asked. "Is that you?"

"Hey, Doc," Butler said, entering the cell. This is your lawyer, Oliver James."

"Mr. Holliday," James said. "The pleasure is mine, I'm afraid."

"I can't shake hands with either of you," Doc said, and showed them the dried blood on his hands.

"Butler has filled me in on your ailment, sir," James said. He turned and said to the policeman, "I want a basin of warm water and some clean rags in here now. This man needs to clean up. He also needs to see a doctor."

"I don't need—" Doc started, but James cut him off with a wave.

"I'll have to lock you in," the policeman said.

"Then do it!" James commanded.

In moments they were locked in and the man went to get the items the lawyer demanded.

"I don't need a doctor," Doc said.

"That's okay," James said. "The more we give them to do the better. As I understand it, we need to keep you here until Bat Masterson arrives with his warrant."

Doc looked at Butler.

"You sent for Bat?"

"He's on his way."

"What are you doin' here?" Doc asked.

"When I left Trinidad, Denver seemed like a good idea," Butler said. "I didn't know you'd still be here."

"I got hot when I arrived here," Doc said. "I never run out on a lucky streak."

"Well, your lucky streak continues," Oliver James said.

Doc laughed, a rough, raw sound, and said, "In here?"

"You have me as your lawyer now," James said.

"Where did you find this fella?" Doc asked Butler.

"As he said," Butler answered, "we just got lucky."

"Mr. Holliday, we need to discuss a few things," James said. "I'm going to help you get cleaned up, get you some clean clothes, and try my best to get you out of here even before Mr. Masterson arrives."

"Good luck."

"Failing that," James said, "we'll keep the legal wheels here from turning too quickly, so that when your friend Masterson does arrive, it won't be too late."

"Well," Doc said, "I guess I'd be much obliged for anythin' you can do, lawyer."

"Let's talk while we wait for the water and the doctor . . . ."

The easy part was getting Doc some water so he could wash the blood and phlegm off his hands that he had spit up the day before. They also got rid of the kerchief, which was unable to accommodate any more, and got him a new one. New clothes would have to come later, and a doctor probably after that.

"They told me they're tryin' to get one to come here," the policeman told James.

"That's fine."

"Also," the man said, "the chief wants to see you when you're finished here." He looked at Butler and added, "Both of you."

"Tell the chief I'll be happy to see him again."

"I'll tell 'im," the man said, and locked them in again.

Doc was drying his hands on a rag they'd brought him, and said, "That's a lot better. Thanks."

"You know the chief personally?" Butler asked.

"Oh, yes," James said. "We've had many occasions to see each other, both professionally and socially. You?"

"I only saw him that one time I told you about."

"Well, it seems we're both about to see him again."

James concluded his conversation with Doc Holliday by assuring him that they'd be able to get him out. "One way or another."

"If there's one thing I've learned about the law over the years," Doc said, "it's that they can trump up whatever charges they want to keep you in jail. But I appreciate your effort, Mr. James."

"When they bring a doctor—and they will," James told Doc, "let him examine you."

"Fine."

James looked at Butler.

"Anything else?"

"No," Butler said. He looked at Doc. "I just wanted you to know you're not alone in this."

"'Preciate it, Butler."

"I've also sent some telegrams to try and locate Wyatt."

"That'd be good," Doc said, "although it does seem like you fellas have things well in hand."

"We'll be back to see you, Doc," James said. "Right now I want to go and see what's on the chief's evil little mind."

CHAPTER 42

Butler and Oliver James were shown to the office of the chief of police. Chief Coolidge did not stand as they were shown into his office. Instead, he just glowered at them.

"Come now, Chief, I know you're glad to see me," Oliver James said.

"Sit down and shut up, James," Coolidge said. "And that goes for your friend, too."

"My name is Tyrone Butler, Chief," Butler said as he sat next to Oliver James.

"Was it your idea to hire this man to represent Doc Holliday?" Coolidge asked.

Butler didn't want to admit it was a bartender's idea, so he said, "Yes, it was."

"And what's your interest?"

"I thought I told you the first time we met," Butler said. "Oh, no, wait, that's right, you wouldn't let me talk. Well, anyway, Doc's a friend of mine, and I don't like seeing him get railroaded."

"Railroaded," the chief said. "There's a legitimate warrant out for Holliday in Arizona for murder."

"There were no murders in Arizona," Butler said.

"Then you live in a fantasy world, my friend," Coolidge said, "where men like Doc Holliday and Wyatt Earp are heroes. Is that it?"

Butler thought a moment, then said, "That's pretty much it, yeah."

"And you," Coolidge said, switching his attention to the lawyer, "what the hell do you think you're doing?"

"The man's entitled to a lawyer, Chief."

"What do you hope to achieve?" Coolidge asked. "Isn't your career already in the gutter?"

"Technically," James said, raising one pudgy finger in his defense, "I've never been in the gutter. I spend most of my time in bars, but I haven't made it to the gutter, yet."

The chief looked back and forth between both of them.

"All I'm trying to do is my job," Coolidge said.

"What about this Officer Mallon, who claims he was in Tombstone?" James asked. "Have you checked him out?"

"And why should I check him out?"

"How about to see if he's telling the truth?" Butler asked. "Doc Holliday says he wasn't there."

"What does it matter whether he was or wasn't there?" Coolidge asked. "Doc Holliday was there. That's the point."

"Look, Chief—"

"I'm going to tell the two of you once," Coolidge said. "Don't get in my way."

"Don't you mean, don't get in the way of the law?" James asked. "Or do you still think that you and the law are one and the same?"

Coolidge got to his feet, his face turning red.

"You haven't changed one bit, have you, James?" he demanded.

"Any reason why I should?"

Coolidge lifted one arm, his own pudgy forefinger extended.

"Get out of my office!"

James stood up and headed for the door.

"Me, too?" Butler asked.

"Go!"

Butler followed Oliver James out of the office, down the hall, and out of the building.

"What does he have against you?" Butler asked when they were on the front steps.

"We've had a few run-ins over the years," James said. "He doesn't exactly hold his men to the letter of the law. He usually just bends it to make things come out the way he wants."

"So what do we do next?"

"I think we should go and find a doctor," James said, "just in case the chief decides Doc doesn't need one."

"Do you know one?"

"I know many," James said, "it's just a question of which one I want to send over. Come on."

"Where to?"

"My office."

"I thought we were going to find a doctor."

"We are."

When they reached the building where Oliver James had his office they stopped in the lobby in front of a directory. Butler then saw why they had come there. There were easily six doctors listed for the building.

"Ah," James said, "there's the one." He pointed to the name Dr. Gerald Healy.

"Is he any good?" Butler asked.

"It doesn't much matter," James said, "but he's about at the same point I am in my career. He can use the business. Let's go to my office first."

Butler followed James to the second floor, to a door bearing his name. The man used a key to open the door, and they entered an outer office Butler noticed had a layer of dust on it.

"I had to let my girl go," James said as they walked through to his own office, which was just slightly better.

"Don't mind the dust," James said. "I haven't been here in a while."

The man went around behind his desk, opened a drawer, and took out a folder.

"I've got to start a file on Holliday," he said. "Care for a drink? I think I've still got a bottle in my bottom drawer."

"No, I'm fine," Butler said. "What about the doctor?"

"He's down the hall," James said. "Give me a minute and we'll go and see him."

Butler walked to the window behind Oliver James and looked down at the street. Coaches, buggies, and cabs went by, and there was plenty of street traffic. He'd noticed during their cab ride that they were on West Colfax Street.

"Pretty busy out there," he said.

"Huh? Oh, I don't notice much anymore."

Butler turned and watched as the man wrote furiously, creating a file for Doc Holliday.

"Okay," James said, "I've got my thoughts down." He stood up. "Let's go talk to Doc Healy."

"What kind of doctor is he?"

"General," James said. "But we want him saying that Doc Holliday is too ill to travel. He's certainly qualified to do that."

"Will he do it just because you ask him to?" Butler asked, following along behind James.

"He'll do it for two reasons," James said, leading the way down the hall. "One, because it'll give him a chance to examine Doc Holliday and two . . . did you see your friend? I believe he actually is too ill to travel."

Now that the lawyer mentioned it, Butler realized he was right. Covered with his own blood and phlegm, Doc Holliday looked like he was one giant step from death.

CHAPTER 43

———◆◈◆———

Gerald Healy was in his office standing at the window behind his desk, hands clasped behind him. His desk was spotless. That is to say, dust but no papers of any kind. Butler assumed the same would be true of his examining room. From behind he was tall and slender, dark hair streaked with gray that curled over his collar. Butler was thinking he was in his early to middle forties.

"Gerry," Oliver James said, "either get away from the window or jump already."

"Ollie," Healy said, "this early and you're not in a bar. Must be somethin' big."

"It is," James said. "I want you to make a house call."

"Where?" Dr. Healy turned and stared at the lawyer. "On whom, and most importantly, why?"

"Well, *where* is at the jail," James said, "and the *who* also answers the why."

"Okay," Healy said, actually turning to face Oliver James, "who?" When he turned, the wrinkles on the face and the potbelly added about ten years to his age.

"Doc Holliday."

Healy stared at them for a few moments, then asked, "The real Doc Holliday?"

"This is Tyrone Butler, he's a friend of Holliday's," James said. "Did you read about him in the paper? About him being arrested?"

"I haven't been reading the newspaper," Healy said. He looked at Butler. "You're a friend of Doc Holliday's?"

"That's right."

"He's got consumption, right?"

"I don't know exactly what he's got," Butler said, "but it's killing him."

"What do you want me to do?"

Oliver James explained that they had a plan to keep Doc from being extradited, but they needed time.

"If you could examine him and say that he's not fit to travel," the lawyer finished, "that would be good."

"It might even be better," Butler said, "if you recommended that he go to a hospital."

Healy looked at Butler.

"You're not thinking of breaking him out, are you?" he asked. "That's not why you want him in a hospital?"

"First of all," Butler said, "I think he probably does need to be in a hospital. And second, no, I'm not looking to break him out. We've got legal means to keep him from being sent back to Arizona."

"We're waiting now for Bat Masterson to show up," James said. "He may or may not still be wearing a badge, which will be helpful."

Healy stared at both of them.

"The real Bat Masterson?"

"Yes, Gerald," James said, "all of these men are real. Do you think you can do this or not?"

"The alternative," the doctor said, "is to remain here,

staring out my window. I haven't had a real patient in months. When do you want me to do this?"

"As soon as possible," James said. "Grab your bag and I'll take you down there now."

"Let me get it from my surgery," Doctor Healy said. "Hopefully, everything in it still works."

As the doctor went into the other room, Oliver James asked Butler, "Will you be coming with us?"

"I think I'll go back to my hotel and see if there are any telegrams from Bat or Wyatt."

"Why don't we have dinner together tonight and we can talk more?" James suggested.

"Fine."

"Uh, by dinner I mean that you, uh, would—"

"Yes, Oliver," Butler said, "I'll buy dinner. Why don't we meet in the hotel bar at around seven."

"And will you invite the lovely Miss Conway?"

"You know," Butler said, "I think I will."

CHAPTER 44

When Butler got back to his hotel he found two messages waiting for him at the front desk. The first was from Bat Masterson, confirming that he was on his way and would arrive in two days. The second was not from Wyatt Earp, as he had been hoping, but from Jennifer. She had written him a note saying she wanted to know what had happened at the jail as soon as possible, and that she would be waiting in her room.

Butler decided to clean up before he went to see her. It would have taken too long to take a bath so he used the pitcher and basin in his room, donned some fresh clothes and walked to her door.

"It's about time," Jennifer said when she opened her door. "I've been wondering what's going on. Come on in." She grabbed his arm and yanked him into the room. She was wearing a skirt, shirt, and boots, looking ready for anything—a walk, a ride, or dinner.

"Tell me," she said. "What happened when you went to the jail?"

"Why don't I tell you over a drink," he said. "We're supposed to meet Oliver in the bar at seven."

"For what?"

"Dinner."

"Dinner?" She touched her hair. "I have to change for dinner."

"You look fine."

"No, no," she said, "I have to get ready. I only have—"

"You have a couple of hours," he said, "and I need a drink. Come on, I'll have you back up here in plenty of time to get ready."

"You know," she said as they left her room, "a man's idea of plenty of time to get ready is a lot different than a woman's."

Butler got a table in the half-full bar, left Jennifer there, and went to the bar for two drinks.

"Brandy for the lady, beer for me," he told Jeremy.

"Comin' up."

"Are you always here?" he asked when the man returned with the drinks.

"Pretty much. How did it go with Oliver?"

"It went really well," Butler said. "He's on the case. I have to thank you for referring me to him."

"Hey, I just hope you can do each other some good," the bartender said. "And I'm glad to help."

Butler returned to the table with the drinks and sat down opposite Jennifer, who was drawing looks from the men in the room.

"All right," she said, "I'm ready. Tell me what went on today, what I missed?"

"Well, Oliver turned out to be pretty good . . ."

"That's amazing," she said when he was done. "I missed all that?"

"You didn't miss much," Butler assured her. "It wasn't pretty, the way Doc looked in that cell. They just let him choke and spit up all over himself . . ." he shook his head.

She reached out and covered his hand with hers.

"I'm sorry your friend was so mistreated."

"On the bright side," he said, "Oliver is getting the doctor in to see him today, and Bat should be here in a couple of days."

She moved her hand up his arm.

"You're such a wonderful man to try and help your friend, this way," she said, "especially since . . ."

"Especially since what?" he asked. "What were you going to say?"

"Well, it's just that . . . Doc Holliday doesn't have a very good reputation. I mean, everything I've read . . ."

"You can't believe everything you read about somebody," he told her. "Especially those dime novels you get back East."

"You must've read some of those while you were still in the East," she said.

"One or two," he admitted, "and then I stopped. My intention was to come west and find out what it was really like. Now I've met some of the men who have had books written about them, and I can see how badly they've been depicted."

"Well," she assured him, "I would certainly put more credence in your opinion than in any of those books. If you think Doc Holliday is worth saving then I do, too."

"Well," he said, "that might be a little dramatic. We're not saving him, actually. I mean, he's pretty sick—"

"But you are saving him from having to stand trial for what happened in Tombstone," she said.

"That's true."

"Although, from what I've heard, the confrontation

was not so much about the law as it was about . . . personal feelings."

"What you heard, or what you read?"

She sat back and said, "You know, you're right. I don't know what I'm talking about. Maybe you should just have dinner with Mr. James alone and I can stay—"

"Nonsense," he said, grabbing her hand now. "He wants you to come to dinner. He asked for you."

"And you?" she asked. "Do you want me to come to dinner, too?"

"Very much."

She smiled.

"Then I better go and get myself pretty."

"That shouldn't take very long."

"You're sweet," she said, standing up.

"Just don't dress too fancy," Butler said. "You'll make us fellas look bad."

He watched her leave the bar, as did most of the other men in the room. Then they turned their envious gazes on him, which made him feel oddly proud.

CHAPTER 45

◆━━◆

"Ah, Miss Conway," Oliver James said as Jennifer re-entered the bar. "What a vision."

The lawyer looked dapper in a three-piece brown suit that showed a little bit of wear and tear on slightly frayed collars and cuffs.

"Thank you, Mr. James."

"Oliver, please." He took her hand and kissed it.

She was surprised. The portly, sorry-looking man she'd met the day before had suddenly become charming.

"Thank you, Oliver."

"Shall we go to dinner? I have a wonderful place picked out just walking distance from here."

"Lead the way, Oliver."

Butler had a feeling that since he was paying for dinner, this place was going to hit him hard in the wallet.

Oliver took Jennifer's arm, entwined it in his own, and led the way down the street.

Chief Coolidge read the telegram he'd received from Arizona. A sheriff and a deputy sheriff were on their way to pick up Doc Holliday. Coolidge found this a relief. He was not at all sure he could have trusted any of his men to transport Holliday all the way to Tombstone. Better to let the state of Arizona deal with it.

But he was also worried about Clint Adams and that damned lawyer, Oliver James. He'd thought himself rid of James, as a result of a couple of cases he lost that he should have won. It had been clear to all concerned—Coolidge, the district attorney, and the judge—that all they had to do was make sure Oliver James lost a few cases, and his ego would do the rest. It had worked like a charm, but now this Doc Holliday thing had brought James out of hiding. That was not good.

He put the telegram in the top drawer of his desk, then got up and left his office. He needed to speak to the district attorney as soon as possible.

At dinner, once they were seated, Oliver James took a newspaper out of his pocket and passed it to Butler.

"Have a gander."

"What does it say?" Jennifer asked.

Butler read it aloud. It said:

> "Holliday has a big reputation as a fighter, and has probably put more rustlers and cowboys under the sod than any other one man in the West. He had been the terror of the lawless element in Arizona, and with the Earps was the only man brave enough to face the bloodthirsty crowd which has made the name of Arizona a stench in the nostrils of decent men."

"That's wonderful," Jennifer said. "It makes him out to be a hero."

"Exactly," James said, accepting the copy of the *Denver Republican* back from Butler.

"I don't know how Doc is going to react to being labeled a hero," Butler said frankly.

"Never mind," James said. "This is a good thing. I had to pull some strings to get this into the paper."

"What about the doctor?" Butler asked. "Healy?"

"Gerry examined Doc," James said. "He agrees with you. Doc Holliday should not be riding a horse—not in his condition."

"And what is his condition?" Jennifer asked.

"He's dying, my dear," James said, "and there's little anyone can do about it."

"Is that what Healy said?" Butler demanded.

"Pretty much."

"What about this place, Glenwood Springs?" Butler asked. "It's supposed to be good for people with Doc's ailment."

"I don't know anything about that, Butler," James said. "I'm a lawyer. Talk to Dr. Healy about that."

Butler decided that he would do just that, first thing in the morning.

Oliver James was in a very expansive mood. He began telling Jennifer tales of his other cases—the ones he had won. She listened with rapt attention, and even applauded him a time or two. Still seated, he executed a little bow.

Having Doc Holliday for a client seemed to have resurrected James. He was vastly different from the man they had seen for the first time with his head almost hanging in a mug of beer. In fact, he was quickly becoming something Butler had never liked—a blowhard.

"Oliver," he said, cutting the man off in mid-story.

"Yes?"

"What are the chances of getting Doc moved to a hospital?"

"None," James said. "Gerry recommended it, but the chief is not having it. He says that Doc has been riding all over the West with the Earps, he doesn't see why he can't remain in a jail cell for a while."

"When are they planning to send him to Arizona?"

"They're not," James said. "Apparently, a couple of lawmen from Arizona are on their way here."

"When will they arrive?"

"That I don't know."

"Jesus," Butler said, "I hope Bat gets here before they do."

"It would be unfortunate if he didn't."

"Unfortunate?" Butler asked. "We have to come up with a plan in case they do get here first."

"I am already thinking about it, Butler," James said. "Believe me, I have everything under control."

As the man went back to telling Jennifer lurid tales of his accomplishments, Butler wasn't so sure he was ready to put Doc's fate completely in his hands.

———◆◆◆———

CHAPTER 46

Oliver James walked back to the hotel with Butler and Jennifer, then excused himself.

"You young people don't want me around bending your ear all night," he said, and bid them good night. He told Butler to come to his office first thing in the morning so they could talk strategy. That fit in with Butler's plan to talk with Dr. Healy.

Butler took Jennifer into the bar, where they sat with their drinks. Instead of brandy tonight she asked for beer, so that was what they both had.

"He's quite a character," she said, about Oliver James.

"Maybe a little too much of one," Butler said.

"What do you mean?"

"I mean he seems to have recovered his confidence awfully quickly, for a man who was in the depths of depression just a day ago."

"What are you saying?"

"I don't know what I'm saying, Jennifer," Butler said. "I'm just not sure I'm going to trust him yet. Not completely, anyway."

"You're still looking out for your friend, Butler," she said. "I think that's wonderful."

Butler looked across the table at her. Without James in the way he could see how lovely she was tonight—and how playfully flirtatious. He began to wonder where this night might lead.

Butler woke in the morning, invigorated. Lying next to him in his bed was Jennifer Conway. It had not taken much to convince her to go back to his room with him. They'd only had that one beer, but she was ready, and so was he.

He had undressed her gently, lovingly, uncovering her warm skin, her curves, her secret places, and exploring them, making them his own. She, in turn, was not exactly inexperienced, something he did not mind in a woman. It made for quite a night.

He examined her in the morning light coming in the window. Her skin was flawless, and even first thing in the morning she was a vision. Mentally, he slapped his forehead for using the same word Oliver James had used the night before.

He started to slide from the bed, but suddenly she had a hold of his wrist. Her strength was surprising.

"Not yet," she said softly. "We're not finished."

"It's morning."

She smiled.

"People have sex in the morning."

She drew him back into the bed.

They had breakfast together in the dining room, and then she went back to her room "to get some rest." Butler went to Oliver James's building, but before going to see the lawyer, he bypassed his office to stop in and see Dr. Healy.

"Good morning, Mr. Butler," Healy said. "What can I do for you?"

He was seated behind his desk, which was still dusty. Apparently, having Doc Holliday for a patient had not been the remedy having him for a client had been for Oliver James.

"Doc, you ever heard of Glenwood Springs?"

"Of course," the man said. "It's a sanatorium right here in Colorado. Why would a young fella like yourself be askin'—oh wait, I get it. You're asking for Doc Holliday."

"Yes, I am," Butler said. "We've heard that the place is helpful to people with Doc's condition."

"Have a seat, Mr. Butler."

He did.

"Of course I've only given your friend Holliday a cursory examination," the man admitted. "I did it for Oliver, and made the recommendations he asked me to. But it's my opinion that's it too late for Glenwood Springs, or any other facility, to make a difference for Mr. Holliday. I think they could probably make his last days more comfortable, but that's what he is headed for, his last days."

"I see."

"Do you?"

"Yes."

"I'm not sure he does," Healy said. "He seemed so unconcerned about everything when I examined him. This man is grossly underweight and undernourished, and it has nothing to do with being in jail. I think sending him back to Arizona to be executed would be a travesty. He's only got a matter of months, perhaps weeks, anyway."

"Well, thank you for talking to me about it, Doctor," Butler said. He stood up and shook hands with Dr. Healy, who seemed surprised by the gesture. "I appreciate it."

"Not at all," Healy said.

Butler headed for the door.

"Mr. Butler?"

"Yes?" Butler turned.

"May I give you a warning, or some advice?"

"Either one would be gratefully accepted."

"Be careful of Oliver."

"In what way?"

"He has always been a man who was out for himself," Healy said. "Some of that changed in wake of his . . . failures, but he seems to me to be on the same path again."

"Thank you, Doctor," Butler said. "I'll keep that in mind."

CHAPTER 47

————◆◈◆————

Butler went back down the hall to Oliver James's office, entered without knocking. Still no girl in the outer office. He walked right into James's office.

"Good morning, Butler," James said from behind his desk. Butler noticed that the surface was gleaming. Could a secretary be far behind?

"I'm reminding myself that you haven't been paid a dime yet," Butler said. "How much would you like now?"

"Will you be footing the bill for Mr. Holliday?"

"Doc pays his own way," Butler said. "He'll pay me back when he gets out."

"Well, then he can pay me when he gets out," James said. "No point in me taking your money."

And as quickly as that Oliver James changed Butler's opinion of him again. Why would the man be requiring no money? What did he care who it came from?

But he still had to keep in mind the warning from Healy, a man who knew Oliver James better than he did.

"That's decent of you, Oliver," Butler said.

"Think nothing of it, my boy," James said. "Now, I

have a few ideas how to keep Doc safe in Colorado even
if Bat Masterson doesn't make it here in time."

"Oh, he'll make it," Butler assured the lawyer. "If Bat
Masterson says he'll be here, he'll be here."

"Yes, but will he be in time?" James asked. "Will he
beat the Arizona lawmen here? That we don't know,
and so we have to prepare for it. I am not disparaging
the name of Masterson. I just like to be prepared."

"I see," Butler said. "Okay, then, you talk and I'll
listen . . ."

A few of Oliver James's contingency plans had merit.
Some were far-fetched. A couple were illegal.

"Wait," Butler said. "Weren't you the one kept asking
me if we're going to break him out?"

"I'm just talking here, Butler," James said. "We're just
tossing ideas back and forth, right?"

No, Butler thought, you're throwing ideas at me. My
idea is that Bat Masterson gets here in time with his
Colorado warrant.

"I'm going down to the jail this morning to make sure
Holliday has some fresh clothes. Do you know what he
likes to wear?"

"Black suits, white shirts, not much else," Butler said.
"Same as me, really."

"Splendid," James said, "we'll do some shopping for
him before we go and see him. I have a tailor who is
actually in this building." He was already going out the
door when he asked, "You wouldn't happen to know
his size, would you?"

Oliver James held the new jacket while Doc Holliday
slipped into it.

"We didn't know your size, but we had some help," he said.

"Help?" Doc asked turning. "From who?"

"It's not important."

Doc looked at Butler.

"Too much meat on your bones, old son," he said. "Who's he talkin' about?"

"Um . . ."

"Come on, spit it out."

"We needed someone who was as . . . let's say, as thin as you, so we, uh . . ." James ran out of steam and looked at Butler.

"We bought a homeless man a meal if he would stand for the tailor to fit him," Butler said.

"Homeless man?"

"Homeless, and emaciated," James said, then stepped back, as if he thought Doc would hit him.

"Was he a drunk?" Doc asked Butler.

"No, Doc," Butler said, "just hungry. We bought him a meal."

Doc adjusted the jacket by shrugging his shoulders and said, "Well, okay, then."

James looked relieved.

Doc had now donned the shirt, trousers, and jacket and pronounced them all as "Fittin' well enough."

"Couldn't do anything about the boots," Oliver James said.

"My boots are fine," Doc said. "I'm obliged for the clean clothes."

"Oh, and these." James produced several new, clean white handkerchiefs.

Doc accepted them and, Butler thought, seemed genuinely touched by the gesture.

"Thank you, both," he said.

"Time to go," the lawman outside the cell said. "You were only supposed to have five minutes."

"Just five more minutes, Eliot," Doc said to the young policeman.

"Sure, Doc," the man said.

"Eliot's okay," Doc said. "He talks with me at night."

"He seems impressed by you," Butler said.

"He's just a good kid," Doc insisted. "Any word from Bat?"

"He's on his way."

"And Wyatt?"

"No word," Butler said. "Might not be any telegraph lines up near Gunnison."

"I wouldn't know," Doc said.

"I've got some motions I'm going to make to a judge to try and delay your extradition."

"You think that will work?"

"I hope so," James said. "I'd hate to be doing all this work for nothing. I'm going to go and see the judge now. Butler?"

"I'd like to talk to Butler for a minute," Doc said, then added, "alone."

"Sure," James said. He looked at Butler. "I'll be at the front door."

"Okay."

Oliver James withdrew and the policeman, Eliot, backed away from the cell to give the two men some privacy. They had taken Butler's gun upstairs, before allowing him to come down to the cell block.

"What's on your mind, Doc?"

Doc turned his back for a minute, seemed to be fiddling with his new clothes again, then turned around and looked at Butler.

"I don't want to die in prison, Butler," he said. "I want to do it outside, preferably with a gun in my hand."

"I don't blame you, Doc, but—"

"Or even inside with a gun in my hand," Doc said, lowering his voice. "You see what I mean?"

"I think I do, Doc," Butler said. The man wanted him to sneak a gun in to him. "I'll see what I can do."

"You're a good friend, Butler," Doc said. "I won't forget."

CHAPTER 48

"Who's this judge you're going to see?" Butler asked when he met Oliver James at the front door of the building.

"His name's Sandburg," James said. "He carries a lot of weight in Denver. If I can get him on our side we just might succeed in our efforts."

"What are the chances of that?"

"Honestly? With Doc Holliday's reputation?"

"Why's that?" Butler said. "I would've thought Doc's rep would work against us."

Sandburg loves everything about the Wild West," James said. "He's afraid to leave his office to experience it for himself, but he'll be tickled to rule on somebody like Doc. And if I bring Bat Masterson into the mix? Who knows? Too bad you don't have a rep for yourself."

"Sorry," Butler said. "I'm just a gambler."

"With friends like Holliday, Masterson, and Earp I'm sure that's not true, but what is true is that you're just not that well known."

"I can't argue with that," Butler said, "and truth be

told, I don't mind it so much. I came West to play poker, not to cultivate a reputation with a gun."

"Well," James said, "the other side of that coin is, with friends like Masterson, Earp, and Holliday, you probably won't stay unknown for very long."

Butler had that same thought himself a time or two.

They decided that it would be better if James saw the judge by himself, so Butler headed back to his hotel. His thoughts drifted to Jennifer Conway and the night they had spent together. It had not been very proper of them to spend the night together, but then who was to say what was proper when two adults agreed on what they wanted to do? When he arrived at the hotel, there was a telegram waiting for him at the front desk. It was from Bat. He had quit the train in favor of a straighter route on horseback, and thought that would get him to Denver late tomorrow.

"Good news, sir?" the desk clerk asked.

"Great news," Butler said.

So good, in fact, that he decided to celebrate with a drink, but not in the hotel bar. Too many businessmen in there for his taste. He left the hotel and headed down the street to find a comfortable saloon.

The shooter watched as Butler entered the hotel, then again as the gambler left. Butler walked north at a slow pace. There was still plenty of daylight so there was no need to rush the shot. There were people on the street, and the conditions were not yet perfect.

He cradled his rifle in his arms.

He could afford to wait.

Butler found a small saloon just off the street, down a

cobblestone alley. The name above the door was Morrison's. The front door was half stained glass but, no matter how Butler looked at it, he couldn't make out what it was supposed to be. To him it was just a bunch of purple, yellow, and red glass. As soon as he entered, though, he knew he had chosen the right place, even though the patrons—all obviously regulars—watched him carefully as he approached the bar.

"You in the right place?" the bartender asked. He was a bulky man with black hair parted down the middle, a broad mustache, and a startlingly clean towel tossed over his shoulder.

"I hope so," Butler said. "I'm looking for a cold beer, a quiet place to sit, and no trouble."

The man eyed him cautiously, then smiled and said, "Yeah, you got the right place."

CHAPTER 49

The bartender—who, Butler learned by listening, was the owner, Tommy Morrison—had been right. He gave Butler a cold beer. He then took it to a back table, where no one bothered him or, after the first ten minutes, even looked at him, which suited him fine. Ever since Leadville, on through Trinidad, and now here, he hadn't gotten much time to be alone. This beer was turning out to be one of the best he'd had in some time.

He looked around at the regulars, studying them. There was no gambling going on, just drinking, conversation, and a lot of laughter. All of these men seemed to be very happy with their lot in life. Butler might have been happy with his as well, what with traveling across the West, making his living playing poker, if it wasn't for that one dark cloud hanging over his head. He couldn't imagine how outlaws did it, living with a price on their heads all the time—but at least they knew who had placed the price on their head. It was a mystery to Butler—a mystery he would go back East and solve some day, but it wasn't time to do that yet.

"You ready for another one?"

Butler looked up, saw Morrison staring down at him.

"I, uh, noticed you was down some," the bar owner said.

Butler looked at his beer mug. He hadn't noticed, but there was only about an inch left there.

"Oh, yeah," he said, "thanks. I'll take another."

"Comin' up."

Morrison went to the bar, returned with a cold mug, removed the inch of lukewarm beer that was left, and went back to the bar without further comment. True to his word, leaving Butler to drink his beer in peace and quiet.

Outside, in the alley, the shooter was waiting. He'd peered in the window to make sure Butler was still there, saw him sitting at a back table, and then withdrew. It would be dark by the time Butler came out. He probably should have taken the shot when he had the chance, but there was no point lamenting that now. He'd just settle back and wait. This was one of his virtues, his patience. It was why he had never missed a target once he set his sites on it.

Once again he cradled his rifle, and waited.

Butler had rarely been in a saloon for an hour without seeing at least one argument, or full-blown fight. And, in some cases, a gunfight. He'd been in this one almost an hour, and nothing.

He was about halfway done with his second beer when he couldn't stand it anymore. He just had to ask.

"Another one?" Morrison asked. He still had that clean white towel over his shoulder. Did he ever wipe anything with it?

"No, I'm still working on this one," Butler said. "I, uh, have to ask a question."

"What's that?"

"It's very calm in here," Butler said, waving his arm. "I'm used to seeing more action."

"You mean like fights?"

"Well . . . yeah."

Morrison shook his head, touched the towel on his shoulder.

"I don't allow no fightin'," he said. "You see this towel?"

"Yes."

"See how white it is?"

"Yes, I was noticing."

"I used to own a place where this towel always had red on it," Morrison said.

"Blood?"

"Yup. I gave that place up, moved over here and opened this place. I don't allow any blood spilt in my place now."

"Uh, how do you enforce that?"

"With this." He reached beneath the bar and took out a club. "Know what this is?"

"A club?"

"It's a shillelagh."

"This is a club from Ireland," Morrison said, proudly. "It's blackthorn wood, the hardest wood you can get."

Butler thought that was oak, but kept quiet.

"It's named after a village in Ireland and, in the hands of someone who knows how to use it, it's deadly."

"And you know how to use it?"

Morrison smiled and it was an evil smile—gleefully evil.

"I'm an expert."

"Well, I'll keep that in mind," Butler said. He tilted up

his mug, finished off his beer, and set the empty on the bar. "Thanks, I really like this place."

"Come on back," Morrison said, "as long as you ain't fixin' to cause trouble."

"I never cause trouble, Mr. Morrison," Butler said, and then to himself added, but it does seem to keep following me around.

He headed for the door, opened it, and was about to step out when he thought of something else he wanted to ask. In fact, he did step half out, just enough to offer the shooter a target, but as the man raised his rifle and fired, Butler took one step back, causing the bullet to miss and lodge in the doorjamb near his head.

CHAPTER 50

Butler threw himself back into the room as the second shot shattered the stained glass on the door. Other patrons in the place looked up at the sound of the shot and broken glass. They all looked at Morrison, and then began to hit the floor. Morrison, on the other hand, picked up his shillelagh and came storming around the bar.

"What the hell—" he roared.

Butler saw that the man was heading out the front door, and tackled him around the legs. Morrison was a thickset man, though, and it was like trying to bring down a couple of tree trunks. He did manage to stop the man's progress, though.

"I know you're good with that thing," Butler said, "but there's a man with a rifle out there."

"Is he after you?"

"It looks like it."

Morrison pointed at Butler with the tip of the Irish club.

"You keep him busy, you hear?"

"I hear."

Morrison broke Butler's hold on him and then headed for the back door.

* * *

The shooter didn't know why Butler had abruptly stepped back into the saloon, but the man had made him miss his shot. He was so angry he took a second, hasty shot, which made him even madder. He had never messed up like this before.

He was now doubly determined to put this gambler in the ground!

Butler drew his gun and moved to the door, crouching low. He crunched the broken stained glass beneath his boots as he reached the door, which was still open. The glass was completely gone, so that there was basically just half a door left. He wanted to use the lower half for cover, but he didn't know if it was thick enough to shield him from a bullet. Finally, he decided he just had to step out, because he was supposed to be keeping the shooter busy. Whatever Morrison was planning, Butler couldn't let the man get killed trying to help him.

He had fallen back onto his heels, so he made an adjustment, got into a crouched position, cocked the hammer on his gun, and then sprang out into the alley, his gun ready. As he did he heard a couple of sounds. First, what sounded like a melon hitting the ground, then a grunt and, finally, what sounded like a sack of potatoes hitting the ground.

He pointed his gun down the alley, but all he saw was Morrison standing there, slapping his left palm with his shillelagh. At his feet lay a man, unmoving, with a rifle next to him.

Butler walked down the alley to join the bar owner in staring down at the man, who looked quite dead. His skull had been split and rivulets of blood were running between the cobblestones.

"Wow," Butler said. "You hit him hard."

"I don't use this unless I mean it," Morrison said.

Butler bent down over the man to check him, then straightened, holstering his gun. "He's dead."

"You know him?"

Butler studied the man's face.

"No."

"Well, he broke my glass," Morrison said, "shot up my place. I told you, I don't allow that."

"Yes, you told me," Butler said.

Morrison suddenly prodded Butler in the chest with the end of the deadly club.

"Don't come back."

"What?"

"You heard me," the big man said. "Don't come back to my place. I don't want trouble here."

"I didn't come looking for trouble."

"Well, it found you in my place, and now I gotta pay."

"I'll pay for the glass," Butler said.

"Yeah, you will," Morrison said, "but I still don't want you comin' back."

"Fine. I'll just wait here and talk to the police."

"You don't gotta," Morrison said. "I killed him, I'll talk to the police."

"I was a witness—"

"You didn't see me hit him," Morrison said, "and I got the bullets in my door to prove he was shootin'. I don't need you."

"But—"

"He might have some friends," Morrison said. "If they show up I don't want you here."

Butler was thinking at that moment that if Morrison prodded him one more time with that club he was going to take it from the man and shove it up his ass—or die trying. At that moment, though, the man dropped the club down to his side.

"Look, I pay the police to take care of stuff like this," Morrison said. "Just go."

"Okay, fine," Butler said. "I'm going. I just have to do one thing."

He crouched down and started going through the man's pockets. He was wearing clothes that had taken a decent amount of money to buy. First he went through the trousers, then the dark jacket.

"You robbin' him?"

"Looking for something with his name on it," Butler said. He stopped looking, remained crouched. "Nothing."

"I'm gonna send for the police now."

"Yeah, go ahead. I'm done."

As he left the alley Butler figured that this had nothing to do with Doc Holliday. This was just somebody else trying to cash in on that price on his head. It was probably already time to get out of Denver, but he had to wait for Bat Masterson to arrive. Then again, attempts on his life like this usually averaged out to one per location.

He walked back to his hotel without incident.

CHAPTER 51

"Ty?"

Butler stopped when he heard his name, turned his head. Standing in the hotel lobby was Jennifer Conway. He had walked right by her without seeing her.

"Jennifer."

"What's wrong?" she asked. "You look . . . odd."

"Where were you going?" he asked.

"I'm not going," she said. "I'm coming back. I went to dinner. Alone, I might add. I thought I'd hear from you before now."

"I'm sorry," he said. "I needed some time . . . let's go into the bar and talk."

She grabbed his hand and said, "I have a better idea. Let's go to my room."

"Jennifer—" He resisted.

"If you're worried about my reputation, don't," she told him. "We took care of that last night." She tugged on his hand. "Come on."

This time he didn't resist, and allowed her to pull him up the stairs to the next floor.

* * *

After they made love Butler decided to tell Jennifer the truth.

"Somebody tried to kill you?"

"Yes."

"But . . . why?" she asked "Was it because you're trying to help Doc Holliday?"

"It's possible," he said, "but I don't think so."

"Well then . . . why would someone want to kill you, Butler? I don't understand."

"Let's just say when I came west I didn't leave all my troubles behind me," he said delicately.

"You mean that someone from back East, from your home, wants to kill you?"

"It seems that way," he said.

"Did the man have any identification on him? Something to give you an idea of where he was from? Who might have sent him?"

"No," Butler said, "they never do."

She sat up in bed, unmindful of her nudity.

"Always? You mean . . . this has happened before?"

Now Butler felt he had gone too far, said too much.

"It's happened once or twice."

"Why do I get the feeling your idea and my idea of 'once or twice' is not the same?"

"Let's just say I've dealt with this problem before," Butler said.

Jennifer pulled the sheet up to cover herself and said, "I think I need a drink."

"Do you have anything?"

"A bottle of wine in that top drawer on the sidebar in the other room," she told him.

Jennifer had a two-room suite while Butler had a single room. He stood up, donned his trousers, and padded barefoot into the other room to return with the bottle of wine and two glasses. He poured and handed her one, then sat on the bed holding his own.

"I just have to absorb all of this," she said. "On top of being friends with people like Bat Masterson and Doc Holliday, you also have a price on your head—"

"Not a legal price," he said, interrupting her.

"But a price, nevertheless," she said, "put there by someone from the East who you don't know. Is that it?"

"Essentially," he said, "yes, that's it."

She sipped her wine.

"Would you like me to go?" he asked. "I don't want you to feel like you're in danger."

"Oh," she said, looking at him, "I don't feel like I'm in danger. I'm just wondering if I'm ready to step into your world. Not that I'm afraid to, just . . . am I ready to?"

"I guess you'll have to find that answer for yourself."

She thought a moment, sipped her wine, then asked, "Can I write about this?"

"No," he said right away.

"Why not?"

"You have to understand," he said. "I'm on the run, until I decide to go back and find out just who is behind . . . all of this." He had not told her the part about some of his family members being killed. "These attempts take place randomly, when someone either recognizes me, or has actually been looking for me and finds me. But if you write about this, saying where we were when we spoke, it gives them more of a starting point. I mean, it's bad enough I have a target on my back, we don't have to make it bright red and flashing, like lightning."

"I understand your concern," she said, "but I assure you, I could write about this without mentioning your name."

"Even a thinly veiled account of what I've told you would be dangerous," he said, "to you as well as to me."

"How so, to me?"

"Someone might come looking for you, figuring you can lead them to me," he said. "And they wouldn't ask nicely."

"I see . . ."

"I hope you do," Butler said. He stood up and started to get dressed.

"You don't have to go," she said.

"I think I'd better," he said. "You need time to think and, frankly, so do I."

He went back to his room thinking that he foolishly might have told her too much. That plus the attempt that already had been made might mean that it was time to leave town. He didn't want to leave, however, until Bat arrived. He hoped that would be tomorrow.

CHAPTER 52

━━━◆━━━

Butler woke the next morning remembering his promise to Doc Holliday to get him a gun. Then he wondered, did he actually promise to get him one, or did he say he'd do what he could? He thought that Doc wanted the gun not to break out, but to take his own life if it looked like he was going to go to jail. How ironic that a man who was surely dying would want to take his own life, but Butler thought he knew how Doc felt. If you're going to waste away you obviously want to do it on your own terms, not locked in a cell.

If he was going to try to slip Doc a gun, it was going to have to be a small one. This last time he and Oliver James had gone into Doc's cell they had frisked James, but had taken Butler's holstered sidearm away from him without searching him further. If he'd had a derringer in his boot he could have given it to Doc and no one would have been the wiser. That seemed to be the way to go.

He had no meeting scheduled with the lawyer that morning or afternoon, so he decided that after breakfast he'd go shopping for a derringer. A small, two-shot variety would be enough, he thought, for Doc Holliday's purpose.

* * *

Butler found a gun shop near his hotel and purchased
a two-shot derringer that would fit into his boot nicely.
He decided, however, not to try to give it to Doc that
same day. Why take the chance of getting caught and
tossed into a cell the same day Bat Masterson was supposed to arrive? Besides, as a lawman Bat might be able
to smuggle the gun in even easier than Butler. There was
still a chance they might search him, but they might not
search a badge toter at all.

Butler returned to his hotel with the derringer. In his
room he secreted it several ways in his boot until he
was comfortable with it. When he was done he looked
around his room. As nice as it was, he wondered how
Jennifer—who claimed to be a lowly writer—could have
afforded a two-room suite. Sure, she said she had some
money put away so she could travel, but even Butler—
who traveled for a living—didn't spend large wads of it
at a time, unless he was particularly flush. The stay in
this hotel must have been costing her a bundle.

Butler wondered if he could trust her? What could
he do if she went ahead and wrote her story, anyway?
DATELINE DENVER: YOUNG GAMBLER FROM THE EAST
RUNNING FROM ASSASSINS. How many flags would that
raise back in Philadelphia? Denver would be overrun by
bounty hunters.

He hoped that she would honor his request and not
write the story. Or, at least, let him know she was writing it so he could head out, get as far away from Denver
as possible. He didn't know her all that well, so there
was no telling what she would do.

Butler decided to go and see Oliver James. He left a
message at the front desk for Bat Masterson in case he

showed up while he was gone, giving him the lawyer's address, and then left the hotel. He quickly got used to the feeling of the derringer in his boot.

As Butler approached James's office the door opened and the lawyer came out, shaking hands with another man.

"I think I can handle this for you just fine, Mr. Lynch," James said. "I'll be in touch."

As the man walked down the hall past Butler the gambler asked, "Are you taking on other clients?"

"A man's got to eat, Mr. Butler," the lawyer said.

"Yeah, but before this you weren't taking clients," Butler pointed out. "We had to talk you into it."

"Come inside."

James went back into the office and Butler followed him. They closed the door behind them.

"Look, you and your friend Doc Holliday have awakened my enthusiasm for my job, which lay dormant for a long time. I'll always be grateful for that."

"That may be so, but I want you concentrating on Doc's case, not taking other cases at the same time," Butler said. "And I don't think Bat Masterson's going to like it, either, when he gets here."

"Which will be when, do you think?"

"Probably this evening."

"So we should be able to get this settled in the next few days," James said. "That's when I'll start work on this other case."

James turned and walked from the outer office into his own. Butler followed.

"What happened with you and the judge?" Butler asked.

"I have a feeling," James said, "we may have to go to the governor with this."

"Why's that?"

"I just found out the Arizona lawmen are in town. A marshal and a sheriff. They're here to take Holliday back."

"And?"

"The judge says their paperwork looks good," James said. "He's not sure Masterson's paperwork will trump theirs."

"Now look—"

"Don't worry," James said. "I'm getting an audience with the governor. He loves the Wild West and all its legends."

"That's what you said about the judge."

"Butler," James said, "it's gonna be all right . . ."

"I hope so," the gambler said.

". . . as long as Masterson gets here today."

CHAPTER 53

━━━━◦◉◦━━━━

"It's about time you agreed to see me," Chief Coolidge said to the district attorney.

"Chief," Daniel Trevor said, "unlike you, I'm an elected official. I've got a lot on my plate. I'm sorry I couldn't see you until now."

"Well, I've got one thing on my plate," the chief said. "Doc Holliday."

"What about him?" Trevor asked. "I thought you were shipping him out of town."

"I'm trying to," Coolidge said, "but he's got friends who are trying to get in the way."

"What friends?"

"A gambler named Butler," Coolidge said, "and, as I understand it, Bat Masterson."

"Masterson!" Trevor said. He sat back in his chair. Coolidge had not been invited to sit, but he did so now. Coolidge was old school, while Trevor was young and on the fast track to the Governor's Mansion. At least, that's what people were saying. Personally, Coolidge didn't think the puissant would be able to handle the job. "It's bad enough we've got Holliday in Denver, we don't need Masterson."

"You mean, you don't," the chief said. "It wouldn't look good for you if Holliday got out, and Masterson was the one to get him out."

"How can he do that?"

"I don't know," the chief said, "but he's a lawman. When he gets here I'm gonna have to show him some courtesy."

"I heard that there's a marshal and a sheriff here from Arizona," the D.A. said.

"You heard wrong," Coolidge said. "There's a sheriff and a deputy sheriff."

"And they're here to escort Holliday out of Denver and back to Tombstone?"

"That's right."

"So, let them."

"I beg your pardon?"

"Give them Holliday."

"I can't do that without a—"

"Look, Chief," Trevor said, sitting forward, "getting Holliday out of Denver can only be good for you and me."

"I don't have an order to turn him over, yet," the chief said. "And his friends—"

"I'll give you an order," Trevor said.

"In writing?"

"Signed, sealed, and delivered," Trevor said. "But here's what I want you to do. Wait until it gets dark . . ."

When Butler returned to the hotel he wasn't sure what his next move was going to be until the desk clerk called him over.

"There's a man waiting in the bar for you, sir."

"What man?"

"He didn't give his name," the clerk said, "but he was wearing a badge."

"A badge? He's a Denver policeman?"

"I doubt it," the clerk said.

"All right, thanks," the gambler said. He tucked the envelope into his pocket and walked to the bar. It only took him a moment to pick out his man because Bat Masterson stood out among the businessmen who populated the bar. Butler smiled and approached his friend, who was standing at the bar.

They shook hands warmly and Butler said, "I wasn't really expecting you until later this evening."

"I rode my horse into the ground," Bat said. "How's Doc."

"Not good. You got your warrant?"

"Right here." He tapped his breast pocket. "I had to upgrade the charge to suspicion of murder."

"Well, their charge is murder," Butler said, "so we'll have to see if that's good enough."

"My warrant is for Colorado," Bat said, "theirs is for Arizona. I think ours will come first."

Butler signaled to the bartender for two more beers, as Bat was almost done with his first.

"Let's take these in the back and I'll try to catch you up on what's been going on," Butler suggested.

"We might have time for me to get down to the jail with my warrant," Bat argued.

"We're going to have to go through the attorney, Bat," Butler said as they left the bar and headed for a table. "And a judge is going to have to rule on the warrants."

"We got a sympathetic judge?" Bat asked.

"Not from the way it sounds to me."

They sat down, Bat with his back to the wall, Butler to the side, so he could keep an eye on the entire bar. He was jumpy because there had already been an attempt on him. If the pattern stuck there wouldn't be another, not in Denver, but he didn't feel like putting his faith into that.

"Okay, then," Bat said, "so what the hell has been goin' on?"

Butler told him everything he knew, including the attempt on his life the night before. He figured the man deserved to know everything. . . .

"These attempts, they happen a lot, don't they?" Bat asked when Butler was done.

"Often enough to be annoying," the gambler said.

"Anything I should know about?"

"Maybe sometime," Butler said, "but not now."

"Fair enough," Bat said, "as long as you know they can happen any time without warning. Adds a little spice to life, doesn't it?"

"Not exactly the way I would have put it," Butler said, "but you're probably right."

"What about this lawyer?" Bat asked. "Any good?"

"Probably good enough for what we need," Butler said. "I don't know that I'd want to go to court with him."

"Sounds like you done a lot for Doc already, Butler," Bat said. "Gettin' that lawyer, takin' him some clean clothes . . . what else is goin' on?"

"Something else you should know," Butler said. "A couple of Arizona lawmen are already here."

"They'll try to take him," Bat said. "We better act fast."

"First thing in the morning," Butler said.

"The lawyer ready?"

"I guaranteed you'd be here tonight, so he's expecting us."

"Guaranteed, huh?"

"Yes."

"Glad I didn't disappoint you."

Butler lifted his mug and said, "Me, too."

CHAPTER 54

Bat was exhausted from his ride. He hadn't been kidding about riding his mount into the ground.

"It died," he said, "when we got to the livery. I hope Doc's life—or what's left of it—is worth that horse."

"I guess that would depend on who you were talking to."

They had another beer, and then dinner together in the hotel dining room. Bat caught Butler up with what had been going on in Trinidad since he left, which had not been much.

"Since you, Doc, and the Earps left there ain't been much goin' on," Bat said. "I think I might be about done there. Ready to be on the move again, take the badge off for a while."

Butler had told Bat everything he needed to know about Doc, so now he filled him in on Jennifer.

"You think she's settin' you up?" Bat asked. "Been settin' you up all along, to write somethin' about you?"

"I don't know why she'd want to do that," Butler said. "She'd be more likely to sell something about Doc, or you, than about me."

"Could be that's been her plan all along," Bat said. "You got to watch out for the pretty ones, Butler."

"I'll remember that, Bat."

Bat decided to turn in early. He'd gotten a room there in the hotel.

"Might as well go first class."

They agreed to meet up early the next morning for breakfast, after which they'd go to the lawyer, Oliver James's, office to find out what their next move should be.

Butler hadn't seen Jennifer all day, but there she was in the lobby now, hurrying over to him.

"Was that him?" she asked breathlessly.

"Who?"

"Bat Masterson."

"Oh, yes, that was him."

"Lucky for Doc Holliday he finally showed up, huh?"

"Yes, it is," Butler said, "or, I hope it is."

She grabbed Butler's arm.

"Do you think he'd sit for an interview?"

"I think maybe you should ask him."

"But . . . do you think he'd do it?"

"I don't know, Jennifer," Butler said. "Bat's got some very firm ideas about pretty women."

Jennifer went on as if she hadn't heard.

"If I could get an interview with him I know I could sell it to a newspaper—maybe even more than one. Is he coming back down tonight?"

"No," Butler said, "he's all done in from riding. He'll be down . . . tomorrow."

He'd almost told her that he was going to have breakfast with Bat in the hotel dining room, but thought better of it.

"And will I be seeing you later tonight, Mr. Butler?" she asked.

"I'm not sure," he said. "I might go out in search of some work."

"You mean a poker game?"

"That's my work," he said.

"Well," she said, "if you don't get back too late, knock on my door."

"I'll do that."

But as she crossed the lobby and went up the stairs he knew he wouldn't. He no longer trusted her, which might have been unfair, but it was how he felt. She was a writer, which was the next best—or worst—thing to a reporter, and you couldn't trust reporters.

He didn't know why he hadn't thought this way before.

Yes, he did.

He decided to check with the head bellman. If anyone knew where a poker game was, it would be him.

Police Officer Perry Mallon unlocked the cell door and said to Doc Holliday, "Let's go."

Doc remained seated on his bunk, wishing Butler had brought him a gun already. He looked up at Mallon, and the other two officers standing behind him.

"Where are we goin' in the middle of the night?"

"You're headed back to Arizona to hang," Mallon said.

"Yeah," Doc said, "if I don't catch a bullet in the back while trying to escape."

"If it was just me you might," Mallon admitted. "But

I'll just shoot you in the knee and drag you out if you don't come." Mallon drew his gun to drive his point home.

Doc sighed. He was going to have to depend on Butler and Bat Masterson having something up their sleeves to counter what was going on now.

"Let's go," Mallon said, cocking the hammer, "I ain't got all night."

"All right," Doc said, standing.

"Turn around," Mallon ordered.

Doc did, and one of the other men handcuffed him that way.

"If we're riding I'll need my hands," Doc told them.

"We'll take care of that when the time comes," Mallon said. "Right now you're walkin' and ridin' a buggy. Move."

"You're not going to get away with this," Doc said.

"We're just followin' orders," Mallon said. "There'll be some Arizona lawmen takin' you all the way back."

As they went up the stairs Doc said, "So we're tryin' to sneak out before anybody misses me?"

"Ain't nobody gonna miss you, Holliday," Mallon told him, prodding him from behind. "Believe me."

CHAPTER 55

Butler met Bat Masterson in front of the hotel dining room early the next morning and they went in to have breakfast.

"Well rested?" Butler asked.

"More than you," Masterson said. "You look like crap."

"I found a poker game last night," Butler explained. "It went on for quite a while."

"How'd you do?"

"I did my business."

"Which means you won."

"That's my business," Butler said.

The waiter came over and they both ordered steak and eggs. They were only halfway through with their meal when Bat saw a portly man come rushing into the dining room.

"Is that our lawyer?" he asked.

Butler turned and saw Oliver James hurrying toward them.

"That's him."

"He's got somethin' on his mind."

James reached the table and asked Butler, "Is this Masterson?"

"Yes," Butler said. "Bat, this is—"

"You both have to do something."

"About what?" Butler asked.

"Doc's gone."

"What do you mean, he's gone?" Butler demanded.

"Just what I said," James answered. "They moved him during the night."

"To where?" Bat asked.

"I don't know," James said. "And they claim not to know."

"Are they claiming he escaped?" Bat asked.

"No," James said. "What they said was they seem to have 'misplaced' him."

Bat looked at Butler.

"They're on their way to Arizona. They probably took him someplace right outside of town, where they'll hand him over to the Arizona lawmen."

"We'll have to go get him," Butler said.

"Yeah," Bat said. "That means we're gonna have to take him away from some other lawmen."

"That doesn't bother me much," Butler said. "I'm not wearing a badge."

"That fact might come in handy," Bat said. He looked longingly at the remainder of his breakfast, then said to Butler, "We got to go now."

They both stood up and hurried from the dining room, leaving Oliver James standing next to their empty table. Just so their money and meals wouldn't go to waste he sat down, combined both plates, and started eating.

* * *

Bat needed a horse, so they went to the livery where Butler had left his and made a quick deal with the liveryman to rent one. Bat had to pay too much, but there was no time to dicker.

Mounted, they rode out of the livery.

"Which way?" Butler asked.

"That's easy," Bat said. "We head for Tombstone. We're bound to catch up."

"Doc asked me to smuggle him a gun."

"Did you?"

"Not yet," Butler said. "I was going to. A derringer. It's still in my boot."

"I've got an extra gun in my saddlebags," Bat said. "When we find him we'll arm him. It'll better our odds."

"If we find him alive."

"The only way we won't find him alive is if he dies on his own," Bat said. "They're gonna want to take him back to Arizona."

"How do we know which way they're going to go?" Butler asked.

"I've made this ride before," Bat said. "There are a couple of good routes. I'm gonna have to make a damn good guess, but if I know Doc he'll be working on a way to let us know."

Doc coughed, hawked up a bloody gob, and spat. It struck a boulder, staining it with red.

Mallon, riding in the lead, turned, and said, "Hawking up a lung, Doc? You feel like fallin' off your horse and dyin' right here, be my guest."

"When I want to lay down and die, Mallon, you'll be the first to know," Doc said. Because you'll be in the ground first, he added to himself.

He brought up another bloody gob and spit it again. Once again it stained a round boulder. No one thought anything of it, except to avert their eyes when he did it.

If Butler and Bat Masterson couldn't see the bloody trail he was leaving, they'd have to be blind.

CHAPTER 56

————◆————

"This guy has got no imagination," Bat Masterson said, shaking his head.

"Who?"

"Whoever it is we're following," Bat said. "He's takin' Doc the most direct route."

"Maybe he's not expecting to be followed."

"An experienced lawman would take an evasive route, anyway," Bat said.

"Then I suppose we're lucky this guy isn't experienced."

"Or he's just plain stupid."

They were a couple of miles outside of Denver, heading due south. Bat had halted their progress to make his observation.

"Wait a minute," Butler said. "How do we even know we're going in the right direction."

"Have you done any trackin' at all?" Bat asked.

"Not if it didn't involve cards."

"Look."

Bat pointed to a rock that seemed to have a dark stain on it.

"What is that?"

"It's blood."

Butler frowned at the stain.

"It doesn't look red."

"It's not fresh blood," Bat said, "and even if it was, it darkens the older the stain is."

"So how old is this stain?"

"Hours."

"So you're saying that's Doc's blood? He's wounded?" Butler asked.

"Not wounded," Bat said. "He's leaving us a trail. You know, like that nursery rhyme."

Butler stared at him.

"With the bread crumbs?"

"Oh," Butler said. "Hansel and Gretel?"

"That's the one."

"That's not a nursery rhyme," Butler said, "it's a—"

"Okay," Bat said, cutting him off, "the point is, Doc's leaving us this trail."

"With blood?"

"Think about it," Bat said. "How do you think he could leave us a trail of blood without anyone noticing a thing?"

Butler thought a moment, then it came to him.

"Jesus," he said, feeling vaguely nauseous. "He's spitting it up?"

"So it's not just blood," Doc said. "It's everything else that comes up when Doc does that."

"Jesus . . ." Butler said again.

"So now all we've got to do is follow this trail," Bat said, "and hope he doesn't run dry."

Bat gigged his horse and Butler followed. Trying not to think about Doc Holliday, Hansel and Gretel.

* * *

"What now?" Doc asked when they stopped.

"This is as far as we go," Mallon said, dismounting. He walked over to Doc, who was not handcuffed in front so he could ride. However, when Mallon grabbed him and pulled him from his horse, he had no way of resisting. He hit the ground with a hard thud that jarred him to the bone and started a coughing fit.

"There he goes again," Mallon said.

The other two officers dismounted and stared down at Doc with distaste.

"This is disgusting," one of them said.

"Who'd wanna live that way?" the other asked.

"He's not gonna live this way for much longer," Mallon said.

One of the policemen looked at Mallon and said, "You ain't gonna—I didn't sign on for no murder—"

"Me neither—" the other stated, but Mallon cut them both off.

"Relax," he said. "All I meant was they'll stretch his neck for him when he gets back to Tombstone."

"Who's takin' him back?" one of them asked.

"We got to wait here for a sheriff and his deputy from Arizona," Mallon said. "The chief's sendin' them here to take him off our hands."

"How long's that gonna take?"

"Who knows?" Mallon said. He pointed to one. "Just start a fire and we'll camp until they get here." And then the other. "You take care of the horses."

"What are you gonna do?" one of them asked.

"I'm gonna make sure our guest is real comfortable," Mallon said.

As the other two walked away he uncuffed Doc,

flipped him over onto his stomach, and then cuffed his hands behind his back.

"Comfy?"

Doc choked and spit up a gob of bloody phlegm in reply.

CHAPTER 57

"No more blood," Butler said.

"You noticed," Bat said. "Good. Maybe that means you're learning."

"It's not a skill I think I'll need in the future," Butler observed.

"Maybe, maybe not."

"The point is," Butler said, "there's no more blood. How do we know we're still going in the right direction?"

"See? You do want to learn."

"I want to know if—"

"Doc only meant to point us in the right direction," Bat said. "If he kept it up he probably would have run dry, or run the risk of having someone figure out what he was doin'."

"Leaving us a blood trail?" Butler asked. "I doubt anyone would have figured that one out. I'm still having a hard time believing it myself."

"Still got that derringer in your boot?" Bat asked.

"Yes, why?"

"I'm just wonderin' how things would've been different if you had already passed it to him."

"Well, for one thing," Butler said, "somebody would probably be dead."

"I'll bet you're right about that."

"Or maybe Doc would've used it to get away."

"And he'd be on the run now," Bat said.

"Wouldn't he be better off?"

"No," Bat said, "because we're gonna get him back and use my warrant to get him out of Denver."

"You sound so sure."

"I am," Bat said. "I'm not gonna let some idiotic Denver lawmen get away with this."

"And what if we run into the Arizona lawmen at the same time we run into the idiotic Denver lawmen?"

"I guess we'll have to deal with them when the time comes," Bat said.

"If it comes," Butler said hopefully.

"Right, if it comes. Come on, we're not too far behind them, and they'll be camping soon."

"Why camp? There's still plenty of daylight."

"I'll explain my thinkin' while we ride," Bat said.

Bat thought that some local lawmen were probably transporting Doc out here to pass him off to the Arizona lawmen.

"They're not gonna want to get too far from home," he finished. "They'll want the others to catch up to them as soon as possible."

"But we're going to catch up to them."

"Right," Bat said, "and, hopefully, first."

Mallon stared across the fire at the other two policemen who were with him. One he knew was named Benson. He didn't know the other one's name. It was true if they hadn't been with him he probably would have found a way to kill Doc Holliday. As Holliday himself said, he probably would have put a bullet in the man's back and claimed he was trying to escape. However, with Benson and the other man along he wouldn't be able to do that.

"Can I get some of that coffee?" Doc asked.

Benson looked over at Mallon.

"Sure," he said, "why not?"

Benson poured a cup and brought it over to Doc. He removed the cuffs, allowing Doc to bring his hands around to the front, then cuffed him again that way. Doc picked up the hot cup and held it in both hands.

"Thanks," he said to Mallon.

"Hey," Mallon said, "I can be a big man. You're gonna be dead soon, anyway."

"One way or another," Doc agreed. "But then, we're all going to die sometime, right?"

"That's true," Mallon said, "but not at the end of a rope like you, Doc."

Doc looked up at the sky. Still a couple of hours of daylight to go. If Bat Masterson and Butler were going to find them they'd have to do it quickly, or be forced to do it in the dark.

"Got anything to eat?" Doc asked.

"We don't plan to be out here that long, Holliday," Mallon said. "Make due with your coffee."

"That's fine," Doc said. "Never hurts to ask."

"I got some beef jerky—" Benson started, but Mallon cut him off.

"Eat it yourself, then," Mallon said. "Coffee's enough for him."

"Obliged for the offer," Doc said to Benson.

He finished the coffee and handed the cup back to Benson, who cuffed him behind his back again. Doc's body ached, not only from the constant coughing spells but from the fall from the horse. He'd been happier in his cell than out here. He was fairly safe there. Out here one of these men could still get it into their head to put a bullet in him—although a quick death from a bullet was much better than some of the alternatives.

CHAPTER 58

Next time it was Butler who raised his hand to halt their progress. They had only ridden about another hour when he smelled it.

"What is it?" Bat asked.

"Coffee."

Bat sat still in his saddle and waited for it to come to him.

"I've got it," he said. "You got a good nose. Smells like it's comin' from dead ahead. Let's go—but slowly."

"Bat, I've got a question."

"Go ahead."

"Why would you come all this way, ride a horse into the ground, risk your life and your badge, for a man you don't even like?"

"I thought we talked about this once before," he said. "Wyatt Earp sees somethin' worthwhile in Doc Holliday. Something even his own brothers never saw. That's good enough for me. Fact of the matter is, you see somethin' in ol' Doc, too, don't you?"

"I don't know that I see something in him," Butler said. "I mean, not anything good or noble or anything like that. I just know I like him."

"Well," Bat said, "I guess that ought to be good enough for me, too."

"Why would you care what I think?"

"Well," Bat said, "you stood with my brother in Dodge, and with me in Trinidad. I reckon if I can trust you with my life and my brother's life, I can trust your instincts about a man, too."

"I appreciate that, Bat."

"Hold up," Bat said, reining in his horse. "I smell it strong now."

"So do I."

"Let's leave the horses here and go the rest of the way on foot."

They dismounted, took their rifles from their saddles. Bat took the lead, Butler following closely, trying to be as quiet as he could. He was nowhere near as comfortable out here as he was at a poker table. Evidence of that fact was that he tripped twice and once sent a rock skittering along.

"You wanna make a little more noise?" Bat asked at that point.

"Sorry."

"Look," Bat said, taking a moment for another lesson, "just lift your feet, okay?"

"Got you."

"Shouldn't we set a watch?" Benson asked Perry Mallon.

"What for?" Mallon asked. "We're waitin' for two lawmen."

"What if somebody else comes along?" the other man asked.

Mallon looked at him.

"What's your name?"

"Daly."

"How long have you been wearin' a badge, Daly?"

"Two months."

"Then don't question me about what we should be doin'," Mallon said. "Or you, either, Benson. Just keep the fire goin' and the coffee comin'. We'll be headin' back to Denver soon enough."

"You know, they're right," Doc Holliday said.

"Why do you even have an opinion?" Mallon asked. "Just shut up."

"I'm just sayin', it makes sense to set up some kind of watch. You never know who might come along—"

"You think Masterson and that gambler are gonna come after you when they hear you're gone?"

"They might."

"I happen to know that Bat Masterson doesn't even like you."

"That makes us even," Doc said. "I don't like Bat much, either."

"Then why would he bother?" Mallon asked.

Doc didn't bother asking Mallon why Doc would have come all the way to Denver from Trinidad and then not go the few extra miles to track them here.

"And that gambler," Mallon said. "Forget about him. The chief is sendin' those two Arizona sheriffs out here. Once you're in their hands—"

"I heard somethin'," Benson said suddenly. He was hunkered down by the fire, across from Mallon, and now he stood up, his hand hovering near his gun.

"I didn't hear nothin'," Mallon said.

"Me neither," Daly added.

"I heard it," Doc said. "Sounded like somebody kicked a rock."

"Yeah, you'd like me to think somebody's out there,"

Mallon said. "It would mean somebody gave a shit about you."

"I tell ya, I heard something'," Benson insisted.

"Then go check it out," Mallon said. "It ain't even dark yet, but try not to get lost."

Benson stared at Mallon for a moment.

"Well, go ahead," the other man said. "You opened your big mouth, now go check it out."

Benson looked at Daly, who looked away.

"Fine," he said. "I'll check it out."

Mallon poured himself another cup of coffee and settled down onto a rock. They hadn't even unsaddled their horses because he'd said the two Arizona lawmen would come along any time. Daly tossed some more wood onto the fire and eyed Doc suspiciously. This was the famous Doc Holliday. He was going to have to try something to escape, wasn't he? Daly had been nervously awaiting the attempt since they left Denver.

"Benson's hearin' things," Mallon said. "He's jumpy. You jumpy, Daly?"

"No, sir."

"Then stop lookin' at Holliday like he's a snake that's gonna bite ya."

"Yes, sir."

Mallon was mad that they'd sent him out here with two inexperienced men. Maybe he should just kill them and Holliday and save everybody a lot of trouble.

CHAPTER 59

Butler pressed his gun against the side of Benson's neck and said, "Not a sound."

Benson froze.

Bat had circled around to come at the camp from the other direction. Once they spotted the fire his plan was to move in fast, because there was no darkness to cover them.

Butler took the man's gun.

"I'm a lawman," Benson said nervously.

"I know."

"Y-you're under arrest."

Butler pressed the barrel of his gun harder against the man's neck and said, "Not today, I'm afraid."

"I'm not alone."

"Stop talking," Butler said. "I know who you are, and I know who you're with."

"A-are you one of the Arizona lawmen?"

"If I was I wouldn't have a gun on you, would I?" Butler asked. "Now I mean it. Shut up!"

"I just want to—"

Butler struck the man on the head with the butt of

his own gun, which he was still holding in his left hand. Benson went down in an unconscious heap.

"I told you to shut up."

Butler tucked Benson's gun into his belt and headed for the camp with his gun still in his hand.

"Where the hell is Benson?" Daly asked.

"I warned him not to get lost," Mallon said. "It'll be dark soon."

"You said those other lawmen would be here before dark."

Mallon made an annoyed face.

"They probably got lost, too."

There was a noise, like a boot scraping, and both men got to their feet.

"Now I heard that," Daly said, drawing his gun.

"So did I."

"So did I," Doc said. "I wonder if it was—"

"Shut up!" Mallon said, pointing his gun at Doc. He looked around. The ground around them was far from flat, with trees and shrubbery and boulders. Plenty of places for someone to take cover.

"Who's out there?" Mallon shouted.

No answer.

"Answer me. Who's out there? Benson?"

Mallon couldn't quite figure out where to point his gun, so in the end he pointed it at Doc.

Bat Masterson, from his vantage point behind a boulder, thought he recognized one of the lawmen in the camp. It took a moment, but then the name came to him. Mallon.

"Drop the gun, Mallon!" he shouted.

* * *

Butler was approaching the camp when he heard Bat's voice call out. Running into Benson had delayed him. He rushed forward, took cover behind a stand of brush, and looked down at the camp. Two lawmen and Doc, who was sitting on the ground, hands cuffed behind him. One of the men was pointing a gun at him.

What happened next was up to Bat.

"Come on, Mallon," Bat called out. "We don't want to shoot lawmen. I'm wearin' a badge, too."

"You're out of your jurisdiction, Masterson," Mallon shouted. "You drop your gun. You got no authority here."

"Well," Bat replied, "we're not in Denver, so neither do you. That puts us at a standoff."

"No standoff," Mallon said. "I got your friend Holliday here. I'll put a bullet in his head if you don't drop your guns and come out with your hands up."

"Go ahead," Bat said, "put him out of his misery. If you kill him I'll be done here. I'll be on my way. And he won't be coughing up any more of his lungs."

Mallon cocked the hammer back on his gun.

Butler believed Bat. After all, he was only doing this for Wyatt Earp. If Doc was dead, there'd be no reason for Bat to stick around any longer. Whether Mallon and the other man dropped their guns, or killed Doc Holliday, this would be over for Bat.

He pointed his gun at the other man, assuming Bat would take Mallon, and waited.

CHAPTER 60

———— ◆ ————

Bat could see the tension in Mallon's body. If he tried anything fancy—like shooting the man before he could shoot Doc—Mallon's finger would probably jerk the trigger even as he was dying. He had to hope that Mallon believed him that he didn't care if Doc lived or died.

"I tell you what, Mallon," he shouted. "Kill Doc, I'll kill you, and the rest of us will go home."

That sounded good to Daly, who lowered his gun until it was pointing to the ground.

"You said you didn't care if I killed him."

"I don't," Bat said, "but I think I'll kill you either way."

"What? Why?"

"Because you made me ride all the way out here," Bat said. "So come on, put a bullet in him, I'll finish you and we can be on our way."

"Wait, wait," Mallon said, putting his left hand out in protest. "Lemme think, damn it!"

"What's there to think about?" Daly asked. "Kill Holliday, already."

"Oh, sure," Mallon said, "then he kills me and you get to go home. You'd like that, wouldn't you?"

"Aw hell—" Daly said. He raised his gun, pointed it at Doc and started to pull the trigger.

Three guns went off at once, and three bullets put Daly down on the ground.

Mallon gave his gun to Bat, then took the cuffs off Doc Holliday.

"Did you bring anything to eat?" he asked Bat and Butler.

"Didn't think of it," Butler said.

"Wait," Doc said, "one of these fellas said he had some beef jerky."

"That was me," Benson said, still rubbing his head where Butler hit him. "In my saddlebags."

"Thanks," Doc said. He looked at Bat and Butler. "I don't suppose you thought to bring some whiskey?"

"Just water," Bat said.

Doc shook his head.

"You fellas are the worst rescuers ever."

They stayed camped there overnight and the Arizona lawmen never showed up.

"I'd like to think they wouldn't go along with kidnapping Doc and taking him back to Tombstone," Bat said as they sat around the fire. "They'll probably still be in Denver when we get back."

Mallon and Benson were trussed up and set off to one side. The body of Daly had been wrapped in his own blanket.

"You mean we've got two lawmen who will stick to the letter of the law?" Doc asked. "What's gonna happen next? Is money gonna rain from the sky?"

"Lucky for you this lawman don't stick to the letter of the law," Bat said.

"Amen to that, brother," Doc said.

The next morning they handcuffed Mallon and Benson with their own cuffs, hands in front so they could ride. They then draped the dead man over his horse. Butler and Bat had both fired when Daly looked like he was going to kill Doc. What surprised them was that Mallon also fired at the man. Mallon had decided that Doc had to live so that Bat wouldn't kill him, and when he saw that Daly was going to kill Bat, he just reacted. He dropped the gun immediately after, and shouted, "I surrender!"

Now he looked at Bat and Butler and said, "Come on, you're not gonna make us ride back into Denver handcuffed, are you?"

"We sure are," Bat said.

"Handcuffed is a lot better than dead," Butler told them.

"He's right about that," Benson said, to which Mallon replied, "Oh, shut up."

Doc, having consumed the beef jerky and half a canteen of water, mounted up as well.

"You okay to ride, Doc?" Butler asked.

"I'll make it," he said, "although I'm tired of feeling naked."

Butler unwrapped Mallon's gun belt from his saddle horn and handed it over to Doc, who strapped it on quickly.

"Jesus," Bat said, "strap on a gun and you even look better."

Doc looked at Bat and Butler. "Shall we go, gentlemen?"

CHAPTER 61

District Attorney Daniel Trevor and Chief Arthur Coolidge were not happy with Deputy Sheriff Linton and Sheriff Paul of Arizona. The two lawmen refused to meet with Perry Mallon and the other officers to accept custody of Doc Holliday.

"That's something that's supposed to happen here," Sheriff Paul said, "in your police station, not out on the trail somewhere."

"You can't just drag a man out of his cell in the middle of the night," Deputy Linton said. "We got paperwork."

"Well," Chief Coolidge said, "we were just trying to . . . streamline the process."

"Chief," the Sheriff said, "you let us know when you have Doc Holliday back in a cell where he belongs. Then we'll come with our warrant."

"B-but . . . Bat Masterson has a warrant as well," Coolidge said.

"Well, we'll just have to see which warrant takes precedence," Sheriff Paul said. "We'll be seeing you, Chief."

* * *

When the chief had given the word to Trevor he exploded.

"You what? You kidnapped Holliday from his cell in the middle of the night?"

"You told me to—"

"I did not tell you to commit a crime, Chief," Trevor had said imperiously. "This office would never condone such a thing."

Coolidge narrowed his eyes. This office, he thought, was not above throwing him to the wolves, was it?

"I'm not takin' the fall for this, Trevor," Coolidge said. "I know people—"

"Chief, chief," Trevor said, lowering his voice. He knew the chief had contacts, and even though he thought his were better, there was no point in getting into a war. "Neither one of us has to take the fall for this. Who actually took Holliday from his cell?"

"Officer Mallon."

"Isn't he the man who first identified Holliday? And arrested him?"

"That's right."

Trevor thought a moment, then said, "I think we have a way out here."

CHAPTER 62

———◆◆◆———

Bat, Butler, and Doc discussed what they should do when they got back to Denver.

"We got a dead policeman and two more handcuffed," Bat said.

"We're going to have to explain that."

"Maybe," Doc said, "I shouldn't even go back. They're liable to put me back in a cell."

Bat looked at Doc.

"I came all this way to get you out, legally."

"With a phony warrant?" Doc pointed out.

"Okay, so it had to look legal," Bat said, "but if you run now they'll hound you."

"He's right, Doc," Butler said. "It's got to look legal."

They were camped right outside of Denver, would be riding in the next day. The two policemen, Mallon and Benson, were off to one side, having been fed and told to turn in. They were still cuffed from behind and slept fitfully, but at least they were asleep. No one wanted their input.

"I don't want to go back into a cell," Doc said. "I may never come out."

Butler looked at Bat.

"You and I still have rooms at the hotel," he said. "We can put Doc in one."

"And what do we do about those two?" Bat asked, indicating the sleeping men. "They'll talk."

"Not if they don't know where Doc is."

"We got to explain a dead lawman," Bat said. "You and me, we gotta stay out of jail."

"Mallon killed Daly," Butler said.

"The man's got three bullets in him."

"Okay," Butler said, "let's think this through. How can we all get off the hook and not go to jail?"

Bat and Doc said it at the same time.

"The governor."

"Right," Butler said. "So we've got to get Oliver James to talk to the governor, while we stay out of sight."

"Not to toot our own horn," Bat said, "but how do you expect me and Doc to stay out of sight?"

"We'll sneak you into the hotel," Butler said.

"And who goes to see the lawyer?" Bat asked.

"I do."

"What if you're picked up?"

"I'll still get to see my lawyer."

"They'll put you in a cell," Doc said.

"Better me than you, Doc," Butler said. "In your condition, you know?"

Doc shook his head.

"I can't ask you to do that," Doc said. "Risk your freedom, your life. Bat risking his badge."

"I'm gonna give it up anyway, after this."

"Still," Doc said, "I should probably just light out—"

"This will work, Doc," Butler said. "We got all night to plan it out."

"And what do we do with them?" Doc asked. "And the dead one?"

"We'll figure that out, too," Butler insisted. "All we've got to do is put our heads together."

"And make more coffee," Bat said. "I'll take care of that."

While Bat put another pot of coffee on the fire to boil—coffee being something everyone took on the trail with them, even if they weren't anticipating that they were going to camp—they continued to discuss their options.

"We could hold these two until we get our freedom," Doc said.

"Trade them you mean?" Bat asked.

"Sure, why not?"

"Because they can charge you for that," Butler said. "We don't need any more charges."

"What if one of us just stays here with them while the others go into town?" Bat asked.

"Who stays?" Doc asked.

"You," Bat said.

Butler didn't like that idea. There was no guarantee Doc would still be there when they came back.

"I think we have to put this in the lawyer's lap," he said.

"That lawyer?" Bat asked.

"He's got a reputation in Denver," Butler said, then added, "at least, he did."

"You think he can figure a way out?" Doc asked. "A way I don't have to go back to jail?"

"I think he's our only way out," Butler said. "He's the one that's going to have to go to the governor."

Bat looked at Doc, who shrugged.

"He did all right by me over the past few days."

"All right, then," Bat said. "We leave it to the lawyer. But I'll talk to him, and you fellas stay in the hotel."

"What about these three?" Doc asked. "We can't have them runnin' their mouths—especially Mallon—until we get things settled."

Butler looked over at the forms of the two sleeping men and the one dead one.

"How about I go in first, then?" he suggested. "You two stay here with these three. As soon as I talk to the lawyer and learn something, I'll come back out."

"And bring somethin' to eat?" Doc asked.

"I liked it better when we were going to the hotel," Bat said.

"Can you figure a way to get the two lawmen into the hotel as well?" Butler asked.

"Like you said before," Bat answered. "We sneak in."

"What about the dead one?" Doc asked.

"We leave him here, cover him with rocks so the critters don't get him. Come back for him later."

"Bat?"

"I'm for any idea where we eat," Bat said.

"Hot food," Doc added.

"Then I think we're all voting for the hotel," Butler said. "We'll leave at dusk, sneak into town and into the hotel, and then I'll go and see Oliver James. Agreed?"

They all agreed and, while there was still a few hours of darkness, turned in.

CHAPTER 63

Early the next morning they all rode in to Denver, but rather than go in altogether. Butler went in ahead to get a head start with the lawyer, Oliver James.

"I'm registered at the hotel," Bat said. "I'll just walk in, and let Doc and the other two in the back way. We'll take them to my room."

"Here's the key to my room," Butler said, tossing it to Doc.

"What about you?"

"I'll just tell them I lost my key. They'll give me another one."

How they used the two rooms was up to them. Butler mounted up, said he'd see them later, and headed for Denver.

Butler rode directly to the office of Oliver James. He left his horse outside, in front of the building, and went in, hoping the lawyer was there. He was.

"Jesus," James said when Butler entered. "Where the hell have you been? Where's Masterson? And Holliday?"

"They're in a safe place."

"You got him back?"

"Yes," Butler said, sitting down in front of James's desk, "but it wasn't easy."

"Did you break any laws?"

"Uh, yeah, possibly a few," Butler said, "but one great big one . . ."

By the time Butler finished his story, Oliver James had both hands over his face.

"Is that it?"

"That's all of it."

"One dead policeman?"

"Yes."

"And where are the other two?"

"Safe."

James dropped his hands.

"What do you expect me to do with this information, Butler?" he asked.

Butler said. "Just get us a meeting with the governor so we can explain everything that happened. We can't explain it to the local law, they won't believe us."

"And what makes you think the governor will?"

"Two reasons," Butler said. "Bat is a lawman."

"And?"

Butler shrugged and said, "Because he's Bat Masterson."

When Butler returned to the hotel, leaving his horse in the livery, nobody in the lobby gave him a second look. Only the desk clerk acknowledged his presence, and that was just with a friendly nod. He was already on the second floor when he remembered he didn't have a key. Rather than go downstairs he went to his room and knocked on the door. It was answered by Doc Holliday, who was holding a glass of amber liquid.

"Hope you don't mind," he said. "I'm drinkin' your whiskey."

"I don't mind, Doc," Butler said, closing the door behind him. "In fact, I'll have one with you."

He poured himself a drink similar in size to Doc's and asked, "Where's Bat?"

"He's in his room with the local lawmen, makin' them comfortable. Did you talk to the lawyer?"

"I did," Butler said. "He shined me on for a while when asked about the governor, but the fact of the matter is he's already got an appointment to see him."

"When?"

"Tomorrow?"

"Can we all go?"

"That's the plan," Butler said.

"So all we have to do is live through this next day and night and we got it made. Nobody goes to jail."

"Well," Butler said, "you won't go to jail, because you had nothing to do with killing that third policeman. That was me and Bat."

"And Mallon," Doc said. "Don't forget Mallon. Who's to say which bullet killed him?"

"That's true enough," Butler said, "but either way, you're in the clear. Once Bat's warrant is recognized, that is."

"This don't seem fair," Doc said. "You fellas come to help me, and now you might be in trouble."

"We just need some cooperation from Mallon."

"Why him and not the other man?"

"Because Benson was unconscious when Daly was killed. The only ones who can say what happened are the four of us. We need a story we can all agree on."

"You, me, and Bat can say Mallon did it," Doc offered. "Shot his own man three times."

"That would be a lie."

"So?"

"The lawyer says we've got to get through this with as few lies as possible. Me, I think we can get through it with no lies."

"None?" Doc asked.

"None."

"You're an optimistic man, Butler."

"I'll talk to Mallon," Butler said. "Make him see that cooperating with us is best. The three of us could pin this on him. I'll make him see that. To keep that from happening he'll agree with whatever story we come up with."

"Suicide, then," Doc said.

Butler laughed, knew Doc was not serious, and said, "I think we'll have to do better than that."

CHAPTER 64

Butler left Doc in the room to go and talk to Mallon and Bat, but before he left he said, "Hey, I forgot. I got this for you."

He pulled the derringer from his boot. Doc had removed the gun belt he'd gotten from one of the policemen. He said it wasn't comfortable.

"Thanks," Doc said, accepting it.

"I was going to slip it to you in your cell, but . . ."

"That's okay," Doc said. He stuck it in his vest pocket, where it fit nicely. "I used to have one just like it. It'll keep me from feeling naked until I can get my own gun back."

Doc was pouring himself another drink as Butler left the room to walk down the hall. When he knocked on the door Bat answered.

"How'd it go?"

"We've got an appointment with the governor tomorrow morning."

"Already? That lawyer works fast. Come on in."

As Butler entered he saw that Bat—like Jennifer—had gotten himself a two-room suite.

"They in the other room?"

"Trussed up nice and tight, gagged, lying next to each other on the bed."

Butler told Bat how Oliver James had already been working on seeing the governor, so they'd lucked out.

"So the governor's expecting the lawyer, but he's gonna get all of us."

"Including those two," Butler said, using his chin to indicate the men in the other room. As he had done with Doc, he told Bat that they needed to come up with a story and have Mallon back it.

"Makes sense," Bat said. "The other guy was out cold."

"So let's untie Mallon, bring him in here and see if we can get him to cooperate."

"Between us," Bat said, "I'm sure we can make him see the light."

"That's exactly what I was thinking."

They went into the other room, grabbed Mallon, carried him out to a chair, and then untied him and removed his gag.

"You men are gonna pay for this," Mallon gasped.

"Mallon," Bat said, "we got a proposition for you, and you better listen good."

"I ain't about to do nothin' for you," Mallon said. "You killed a lawman."

"Did we?" Butler asked. "Or did you?"

"The way I'm gonna tell it—"

"It's gonna be three against the word of one," Bat said, cutting him off. "Now, you wanna listen or talk? Because this is gonna benefit all of us."

Mallon looked stubborn, but then said, "Okay, I'll listen."

CHAPTER 65

When Bat Masterson, Doc Holliday, and Tyrone Butler entered the governor's office with Oliver James they really had no way of knowing for sure if Perry Mallon was going to back their play. All they could do was wait and see.

They were all ushered into the presence of Governor Frederick Pitkin, who stood behind his desk as they came in.

"I want you gentlemen to know that I feel bamboozled by this . . . this turnout. It was my understanding that I would be meeting with Mr. James today."

"It's not Mr. James's fault, sir," Bat Masterson said. "He didn't know that we'd be here, either."

"Mr. Masterson, I want you to know that it is only on the strength of your reputation, and the fact that you happen to be a Colorado lawman at the moment, that I agreed to see you all. Please, find seats."

At that moment the door opened and a man stuck his head in.

"Sir, the chief of police and the district attorney are outside as well."

"Tell them both that I will see them after this meeting."

"Sir, they insist that what they have to say impacts this meeting."

"Governor," Bat said, "I really think that your decision in this matter should rest solely on the facts, and not on what the chief of police and district attorney might have to say."

"Thank you for that, Mr. Masterson, but I do know how to do my job," Pitkin said. To his man he added, "Tell them later."

"Yes, sir."

"Now," Pitkin said as the door closed, "which of you gentlemen will present this case."

Oliver James cleared his throat. He wasn't happy, but he had finally agreed that Bat should do the talking.

"Sir," he said, "we've agreed amongst ourselves that Mr. Masterson should present our case."

"Very well." Pitkin turned his attention to Bat and said, "But first I'd like to be introduced to the other men in the room."

"I'm sorry, sir," Bat said. "This is Tyrone Butler, a friend of both Doc Holliday's and mine. This is a Denver policeman, Perry Mallon. And, of course, Doc Holliday."

Mallon looked away, Doc looked directly at the governor with bloodshot eyes. He had just suffered a coughing fit before they entered the room. Butler thought this would work in their favor. Doc looked awful.

Bat produced his warrant and set it on the governor's desk, then proceeded to tell the man that when he arrived with the warrant the prisoner—Doc—was gone, having been whisked away—"kidnapped"—in the middle of the night, by Denver police who were intent on handing him over to lawmen from Arizona.

"What happened to the Arizona lawmen?" Pitkin asked.

"They would not go along with it, Governor," Bat said.

"To their credit," James inserted.

"Mr. Butler and I went out to bring Doc back," Bat said, and here was where the story got dicey.

According to Doc, Daly, the dead policeman, went crazy, tried to kill Doc, even tried to kill his own colleague, Mallon. This was not far from the truth.

"We all fired at the same time, sir," Bat said. "We have no way of knowing if all three bullets killed him or, if it was one, whose it was."

Pitkin looked at Mallon for the first time.

"Is this true, Officer Mallon?" he demanded.

All eyes were on Mallon, waiting for his answer.

"Yeah—yes, sir, that's how it happened."

Pitkin picked up the warrant and read it carefully.

"Robbing a stagecoach in Pueblo, Colorado?" he asked. "Shooting a man?"

"Yes, sir," Bat said. "Pueblo wants him bad."

"This would seem to supercede any warrant sworn out here in Denver," Pitkin said.

Mallon started to say that the warrant he'd arrested Bat on was from Tombstone, but then shut his mouth.

"Officer, do you have anything to say?" the governor asked.

"No, sir."

"Do you have any idea what your boss, Chief Coolidge, wants with me today? Or the D.A.?"

"To tell you the truth," Mallon said, "I'll bet they're gonna say I took Doc Holliday out of his cell my own self."

"When in fact?"

"When in fact I was ordered to."

"I could bind you all over for trial of the death of Officer Daly," the governor said, "but since you all agree on your story I'm not going to do that." Pitkin handed Bat the warrant. "Marshal Masterson, the prisoner is yours. Do me a favor and get him out of Denver."

"My pleasure, sir."

"That's it?" Doc asked. These were the first and only words he had spoken.

"Unless you have something else to add, sir?" Governor Pitkin asked.

"Oh, no, I've got nothin' to add, sir," Doc said. "Thank you."

"I don't know why you're thanking me, Mr. Holliday," Pitkin said. "The marshal here is going to take you right from here to Pueblo."

"I just don't like Denver, Governor," Doc said. "Too many people trying to do me harm."

"All the more reason you should leave, sir."

"Yes, sir," Bat said, before anyone else could speak, "we're leavin'."

"All of you?"

"All of us," Bat said.

"Hey," Mallon said, "I got a job—"

"Mr. Mallon," the governor said, "the chief and the D.A. are coming in here next. By the time I'm through with them, I don't think you'll have a job. Do you?"

"Uh, no, sir."

"Like I said," Pitkin finished, "I suppose you'll all be leaving Denver."

"Yes, sir," Mallon said.

"Just as soon as we can, sir," Bat said.

"Then, I think we're done here," the governor said.

CHAPTER 66

Bat, Doc, and Butler all decided to leave town at the same time. They had no idea what Perry Mallon had done. The last time they'd seen him was in front of the Governor's Mansion. He'd thrown them all a disgusted look and stalked off.

Through Oliver James they learned that both the chief of police and the district attorney had been replaced, quietly.

"Won't even make the newspapers," James said.

But these were once powerful men who were now out of a job, and they'd blame other people for that. If Bat, Doc, and/or Butler stayed in Denver any longer, they'd be looking for trouble. None of them were afraid of it, but they would all rather avoid it.

Butler also discovered that Jennifer had left town while he and Bat were off chasing down Doc.

"I'd be watching for a newspaper story somewhere, if I was you," Bat told him. "If she left, it's because she got what she wanted."

"I won't see it," Butler said. "I don't make a habit of reading newspapers from all over the country."

"Don't worry," Doc said, "if there is a story, somebody will let you know."

Oliver James had met the three of them for breakfast and had presented them with his bill. Butler and Doc decided to split it, even though Doc was insisting the expense should be his.

"You didn't ask for my help," Butler pointed out, "didn't ask for me to bring a lawyer into the situation."

"I don't much care who pays me," James had said, "as long as I get paid."

Instead of putting the lawyer off and "sending" him his money, Bat and Doc settled with him and they shook hands.

"I owe you a debt of gratitude," he told Butler as they were shaking hands.

"For what?"

"Like I told you, you rekindled my interest in the law. I thank you for that."

After James left the three men split another pot of coffee, and then they headed for the livery together, where their horses—including a new one that Bat had purchased—were saddled and waiting.

"Where you headed, Doc?" Bat asked.

"Don't know for sure," Doc said. "Away from here."

"Glenwood Springs?" Butler asked.

Doc hesitated, then said, "Maybe."

They walked their horses outside. Doc shook hands with both men, mounted his animal, and left. Before riding off, though, he said something to Butler that was similar to what Oliver James had said.

"I owe you—and I don't forget."

"Good enough for me, Doc," Butler said.

"Thanks, Bat," Doc added.

"Sure, Doc."

He turned to leave, then turned back to Bat.

"How'd you come up with that Pueblo warrant?"

"They had a highwayman operatin' around there for a while. Never caught him." Bat shrugged.

"So now I'm a highwayman," Doc said.

"Not unless somebody wants to execute that warrant," Bat told him, "and that ain't gonna happen."

They watched him ride off.

"Wonder how much time he's got left?" Bat said aloud.

"Don't know," Butler said. "Guess that depends on whether or not he goes to Glenwood Springs."

Bat looked at Butler and asked, "And you? Where are you headed?"

"California, I guess."

"San Francisco?"

"Most likely."

"Maybe I'll see you there," Bat said. "I got to go back to Trinidad to settle up and turn in my badge. After that . . . who knows?"

They rode out of Denver together, until a certain point, where Bat would continue south and Butler would head west. Bat put his hand out and Butler shook it.

"Until next time," the legend said.

"I look forward to it, Bat," the gambler said.

Butler watched Bat ride off, and once the man topped a rise and disappeared from sight on the other side, he gently gave his horse his heels and headed off.